TWICE A FATHER

Widowed dad Reeve Walker was shocked to discover he had another daughter — a child he'd never known existed. His little girl had become friends with her own half sister, without anyone knowing the truth. Anyone, except Shay O'Brien, his secret child's mother ... Shay had loved Reeve, but she had her reasons for keeping their daughter from him. Now, the marriage proposal she'd once dreamed about had finally come true. Even if it was to be a marriage of convenience ...

MOYRA TARLING

TWICE A
FATHER

Complete and Unabridged

LINFORD
Leicester

First published in
the United States of America in 1996

First Linford Edition
published 2012

British Library CIP Data

Tarling, Moyra.
  Twice a father. - -
  (Linford romance library)
  1. Love stories.
  2. Large type books.
  I. Title II. Series
  823.9′2–dc23

  ISBN 978–1–4448–1111–7

Published by
F. A. Thorpe (Publishing)
Anstey, Leicestershire

Set by Words & Graphics Ltd.
Anstey, Leicestershire
Printed and bound in Great Britain by
T. J. International Ltd., Padstow, Cornwall

This book is printed on acid-free paper

To my brothers:
Al, Bob and Ian.
Thanks for the love and the laughter.
Long may it continue.
Sis

Fabulous Fathers

Dearest Emma,
As I watch you building castles in the sand I find it hard to believe just how quickly you've grown. From the moment I first held you in my arms I was blown away by the emotion that overwhelmed me as I gazed down at your perfect features. And when you curled your tiny hand around my finger and hung on tight I vowed I would always be there for you.

You have brought so much love and joy into my life since that first day that I thank my lucky stars I was chosen to be your father. I'd never realized the importance of fatherhood or just how difficult a job it is. Having a daughter has enriched my life in so many ways that when I found out Mandy was my daughter, too, my reaction went from surprise

1

to joy to wonder. Mandy is like you in so many ways, Emma. She is beautiful and bright and warm and loving and as easy to love as the woman who gave birth to her.

Once a father, twice a father! Hmm ... I'm feeling a bit out-numbered here. I wonder what my girls would say to thrice a father!!!

Love,

Dad

1

'From this day forward . . . '

Shay O'Brien sat in the rear of the tiny chapel and listened to the voice of Reverend Hardcastle as he solemnly spoke the wedding vows to the couple in front of him.

Shay barely heard her aunt's friend, Alice, repeat the words to her husband-to-be, Dr. Charles Walker, general practitioner and longtime resident of Stuart's Cove, a small town on the west coast of Vancouver Island. It was the second marriage for both Alice and Charles, and Shay felt a twinge of envy for the couple who had found such happiness in each other in the autumn of their lives.

Shifting her gaze to the child standing beside the couple, Shay felt her heart swell with pride and her eyes fill with tears at the sight of her nine-year-old daughter, Amanda. A tomboy through and through, Mandy felt more at home in a T-shirt and shorts or her favorite blue jeans, with her dark brown hair pulled back into a ponytail.

But today, Mandy was dressed in a beautiful pink floral dress and shiny black leather shoes, and looked almost as pretty as the bride. A smile curled at the corner of Shay's mouth as she watched her daughter shift restlessly from one foot to the other.

Suddenly, there was a soft swish of sound behind her as the chapel door opened, and Shay turned to glance at the latecomer.

Her breath caught in her throat as the man's face came into sharp focus. Reeve? No, it couldn't be! He wasn't supposed to be here, she told herself, remembering the guilty relief she'd felt when Alice had said Charles's son wouldn't be attending the wedding.

Shay felt her pulse pick up speed and she closed her eyes, praying silently that she was mistaken, that the man dressed in a blue blazer and gray slacks only looked like Reeve.

But a moment later, she knew there was no mistake. Her heart lurched painfully inside her breast as she gazed at the incredibly handsome and utterly unforgettable features of Reeve Walker, the man who ten years ago had changed her life forever.

As Shay fought to control her wayward response, she realized with a start that Reeve wasn't alone. Another figure had slipped through the open door with him, a smaller figure . . . that of a child. For the second time in as many minutes, Shay's lungs forgot how to function as she found herself staring at Reeve's daughter, Emma, Mandy's half sister.

Shay had only learned of Emma's existence two months ago during a visit to Dr. Walker's clinic when Mandy had needed treatment for a flu virus.

Dr. Walker had been chatting to Mandy, putting the child at ease while he examined her. He'd casually commented about his own six-year-old granddaughter, Emma, saying he wished she didn't live so far away in New York.

Foolishly, Shay had never even considered the possibility that Reeve might have other children. But ever since she'd fled from Stuart's Cove ten years ago, she'd tried not to think about him at all. It had been an impossible task, of course, especially after Amanda was born. She only had to look at the child they'd created together to remember the man she'd loved with all her youthful heart.

She recalled feeling apprehensive and upset the day she decided to call Reeve. It wasn't every day she telephoned a man on the other side of the country to tell him she was pregnant with his child.

Charles had told her Reeve was staying in New York at the home of a friend, another medical student, whom he'd met while attending university.

After dialing the number, Shay had waited in nervous anticipation for someone to answer.

What Reeve's father had omitted to mention was that the medical student his son was staying with was a woman.

Nonetheless, Shay had politely requested to speak to Reeve. Her request had been met with the sound of soft laughter.

'Oh . . . you want to talk to the man I'm going to marry, do you?' the voice on the other end had responded with wry amusement, before adding, 'Reeve, darling . . . it's for you.'

The telephone receiver had fallen from Shay's hand. Dazed, she'd stared at the instrument as if it were an alien from outer space. Through the haze of pain engulfing her, she'd suddenly heard Reeve repeatedly saying, 'Hello?' Stifling a sob, she'd gingerly lifted the receiver and returned it to its original resting place.

Annoyed at the route her thoughts had taken, Shay brushed away the memory, conscious all the while of the two people seated next to her. Glancing at the child wearing a pretty pink and white sundress and clutching a bedraggled rag doll, Shay felt herself grow tense. She wanted to dislike her, wanted to find something unlovable about her, simply because unlike Mandy, Emma had been fortunate enough to have enjoyed the love and support of a father all her young life.

But gazing at the short dark brown curls the same color as Mandy's, together with her cherublike features, Shay couldn't seem to drum up any negative emotions. And when the little girl lifted her eyes briefly to meet hers, Shay felt a pain clutch at her heart.

Emma's eyes were the same corn-flower blue as Mandy's, but instead of seeing a glint of childish mischief or a twinkle of playful humor in their depths, Shay glimpsed only a look of anguish and profound sadness.

It was all Shay could do not to put her arm around the child and ask her why she looked so sad. But she curbed the impulse and turned her attention to Reeve sitting at the other end of the pew.

Shay studied his handsome profile. His hair was still the color of polished mahogany and his features, forever etched in her heart, held the same dark brooding quality of a hero in a romantic novel.

As she continued to gaze at him, she noticed the lines of worry around his mouth, and the tension in his jaw. A frisson of sensation scampered down her spine. Something was wrong. She could see it in Reeve's face and in the taut lines of his body.

But before she could even begin to speculate on the reason behind the tension, a commotion at the front of the chapel brought Shay's attention back to the ceremony. Glancing up, she saw Mandy, down on her hands and knees, groping around on the floor.

Before anyone could react, Mandy leaped to her feet once more. 'It's okay! I've found them!' Triumphantly, she held up the rings for everyone to see and, oblivious to the smiles and subdued laughter her antics had generated, handed the rings to Reverend Hardcastle before quickly moving back to her place next to Alice.

Shay sighed and shook her head. She tried, for the remainder of the ceremony, to concentrate on the service and the couple exchanging rings, but found her thoughts straying continually to Reeve and Emma. The feeling that something was wrong continued to nag at her.

Where was Louise? Shay suddenly wondered. Why hadn't Reeve's wife accompanied him and their daughter for her father-in-law's wedding?

As the organist began to play, filling the chapel with the resounding tones of Mendelssohn's 'Wedding March,' the group of friends and neighbors gathered to celebrate the wedding of Dr. Charles Walker to Alice Carmichael rose as the smiling couple made their way down the aisle.

Charles was the first to spot his son, and Shay watched as the older man's eyes lit up.

'Reeve . . . my boy. How wonderful to see you,' Charles exclaimed as he and Alice drew level with them. 'Darling, look who's here.' He flashed his new bride a smile.

'Reeve, we're so glad you changed your mind,' Alice said, leaning forward to give her new stepson a kiss on the cheek. 'Oh . . . and this must be Emma.' She looked to the child practically hiding behind her father.

Trapped on the inside of the pew, Shay had little option but to watch the reunion, noting with a frown that Emma neither smiled nor responded in any way to the greeting she received from Alice.

Charles threw his son a startled look. 'You brought Emma?' he said, his smile growing brighter. 'Does that mean . . . ?' he began, but at the warning glance Reeve bestowed on him, Charles quickly ground to a halt.

'It means we changed our minds,' Reeve responded smoothly.

Charles nodded and smiled at his granddaughter. 'All I can say is Alice and I are thrilled that you're here.'

Shay watched as Emma lifted her gaze to look at her grandfather, but again there was no answering smile, no glimmer of response. In fact, her small face remained devoid of expression.

'Don't be shy, Emma.' Reeve's tone was soothing. 'You remember your grandfather, don't you?' he coaxed gently.

Tightening her hold on her doll, Emma shook her head and lowered her gaze before retreating several steps, only to collide with Shay.

'Oops . . . careful,' Shay cautioned softly, causing the child to gasp in surprise and turn wide-eyed to look up at Shay.

'Charles, dear, we're holding up the proceedings,' Alice noted, effectively diverting attention away from Emma.

A quick glance behind him served to

confirm that fact. 'You're right,' Charles acknowledged. 'We'd better move on. The reception is in the hall right next door,' he told Reeve. 'We'll see you there in a few minutes.' Taking his wife's hand, they moved through the open doors of the chapel.

The organist continued to play as the remaining wedding guests followed the bride and groom into the late-afternoon summer sunshine. Reverend Hardcastle, who was holding on to Mandy's hand, nodded first to Reeve then to Shay before following the procession making its way outside.

As the last of the guests exited, Shay was suddenly aware that Reeve had turned to look at her, a frown of puzzlement on his handsome face.

'Shay? Good heavens! I hardly recognize you,' he said, his gray eyes flicking over her with interest.

'Hello, Reeve. It's been a long time,' she said lightly, trying to decide whether or not she should be pleased or insulted that he hadn't recognized her.

'It must be close to ten years,' he replied as he captured his daughter's hand and urged her into the carpeted aisle.

'At least,' Shay said evenly. 'I gather this is your daughter,' she continued as she joined them.

'Yes, this is my daughter, Emma,' he confirmed, and hearing the unmistakable pride and love in his voice, Shay felt a pain tug at her heart.

'Hello, Emma. It's nice to meet you.' Shay smiled at the little girl who kept her gaze pinned to the floor, ignoring the greeting.

'Emma is a bit shy. She doesn't like to talk very much,' Reeve said as he waited for Shay to proceed.

Shay edged past him, careful not to make contact, thinking that while Emma's behavior could indeed be construed as merely shyness, Shay instinctively sensed that something was wrong.

'My father mentioned that you'd come back to Stuart's Cove,' Reeve said as they walked along the sidewalk, with Emma between them. 'You have a daughter, too, I hear,' he commented as they reached the door to the tiny hall adjacent to the chapel.

Shay felt her heart kick against her rib cage at his words and moistened lips that were suddenly dry. 'Yes, I do,' she managed to say, glad that she didn't have to meet his gaze.

'What's her name?' Reeve asked.

Shay swallowed the lump of emotion suddenly clogging her throat. 'Amanda. Though she much prefers to be called Mandy,' she replied, relieved that her voice betrayed none of the anxiety rippling through her.

'That's a pretty name,' Reeve commented. 'Was that Mandy at the front of the chapel by any chance?'

A feeling of panic assailed her. Had he guessed? Did he know Mandy was his daughter? That would certainly explain the tension she'd sensed in him.

'Ah . . . yes, that was Mandy,' Shay responded after a lengthy pause.

'I thought I could see a resemblance,' Reeve said as they continued along the sidewalk. 'I was sorry to hear about your aunt.'

'Thank you,' Shay responded, relieved that he'd switched topics and touched by the compassion she could hear in his voice.

'My father tells me you're planning to reopen your aunt's bed-and-breakfast inn,' he commented. 'What does your husband think about putting down roots in Stuart's Cove?' Reeve asked as they came to a halt outside the door of the hall.

'I'm not married.' She noted the startled glance she received from the man beside her. 'It was nice to see you again, Reeve. If you'll excuse me. I'm catering this affair, and there are a few things I need to see to in the kitchen.' She turned and walked away.

Reeve stood for several seconds and watched Shay disappear from sight. He'd been astonished to discover that she'd been sitting with them at the rear of the chapel, but he'd been preoccupied with his own thoughts and hadn't given the other occupant of the pew much more than a cursory glance.

But the moment she'd spoken, he'd instantly recognized the husky tones of her voice. She'd changed . . . grown up. Gone was the wide-eyed and passionate eighteen-year-old he remembered, and in her place was a mature woman, a woman with more than a touch of sophistication about her.

And she was beautiful. Stunningly so, in fact.

Reeve smiled to himself. Shay had been ten years old and he sixteen when she'd come to live next door with her aunt. From that time on, she'd looked on him as an older brother. She'd confided in him that she despaired of ever developing curves in the right places or of having a boyfriend of her own. Though he'd tried to reassure her, she'd never believed his prophesy that she would one day turn into the proverbial swan.

There was a definite satisfaction in the knowledge that he'd been right. Those long legs, encased in silk stockings, were shapely indeed, and the navy and white full-skirted dress she was wearing accentuated her hips, her narrow waist and high, firm breasts. Her light brown hair still sported those fiery flashes of red she'd always hated and though cut shorter than he remembered, was styled to curl seductively just below her jawline.

Was it really ten years since he'd last seen her? Reeve frowned, remembering with a mixture of guilt and regret that summer's night so long ago. It was a memory he'd never quite been able to banish from his mind. A memory that had the power to stir him, even now.

Because there had been nothing brotherly about the emotions she'd aroused in him that night as he'd walked her home from her graduation dance at the local high school. He still wasn't sure at what moment things had gotten out of hand. What he did remember clearly was that they'd made love, passionate love, under a starry sky.

'Reeve. Over here, son.'

At the sound of his father's voice, Reeve was jolted out of his reverie. Pushing the disturbing memory to the back of his mind, he turned and, still holding Emma's hand, began to make his way toward the newlyweds.

As they reached the head table, Reeve felt Emma tug her hand free and move behind him to clutch at the bottom of his suit jacket. With a sigh, he wondered if bringing Emma to Stuart's Cove would prove to be a waste of time.

'Sit down, Reeve. Emma, you can sit beside your daddy,' Charles Walker suggested, smiling at his grand-daughter.

Reeve gently lifted Emma into the chair before folding himself into the seat next to his father.

Leaning across the table, Reeve addressed his new step-mother, 'Alice, I'd like to apologize for not letting you know we were coming. I hope we haven't upset the proceedings too much by showing up out of the blue like this.'

'Don't be silly,' Alice admonished kindly. 'Your father and I are so pleased that you're here,' she went on graciously.

'What changed your mind?' Charles asked, joining the conversation.

Reeve leaned back and smiled. 'Well, it isn't every day a son gets the opportunity to watch his father get married,' he replied easily. Much as he wanted to tell his father the real reason for his appearance, now was not the time or place to say more. 'I thought Emma might enjoy a change of scenery. Being cooped up all day in a Manhattan apartment in July isn't much fun for a six-year-old.'

'I suppose not,' Charles commented, though Reeve could see that his father longed to question him further about Emma.

'I'll bring you up to date later, Dad,' Reeve added quietly just as one of the waitresses began to serve salad to those seated at the head table.

Reeve turned and glanced at Emma, who appeared to be oblivious to her surroundings as she played with her rag doll. A rush of love washed over Reeve as he watched his daughter. Not for the first time he sent up a silent prayer that someday in the very near future he would hear her call him daddy once again; hear, too, the tinkling sound of her laughter, and see again her heart-stopping smile.

Since his divorce from Louise two years ago, he'd seen Emma at the whim of his ex-wife, who refused to comply with the visitation rules set down by the court. Bitter and angry that he'd actually had the audacity to leave her, Louise had perversely enjoyed sabotaging his plans to see Emma, canceling his visits on short notice with a lame excuse, simply as a means of extracting some kind of revenge.

Knowing the adverse effect their fights had on Emma, Reeve had chosen not to pursue the matter. But he'd found it hard to live with the guilt he felt at not being allowed to spend more time with his daughter, and there had been times when he'd grown fearful Louise would turn Emma against him.

But those days were over. Louise was dead. Killed in a car accident a little over three months ago. Emma had been a passenger in the car with her mother, but by some miracle had survived the crash with little more than a few scratches. Yet while Emma appeared to be the same little girl he loved to distraction, emotionally the accident had taken its toll. In the aftermath, Reeve had been granted custody of his daughter, but there was little joy in having a daughter who looked at him as if he were a total stranger.

As a doctor himself, he'd treated numerous patients who'd reacted in a similar fashion after being involved in a traumatic accident. But this time, the patient was his own flesh and blood, and the level of frustration and feelings of helplessness he'd experienced had intensified a hundredfold.

He'd been told repeatedly that all she needed was time, that the trauma of the crash would slowly begin to fade from Emma's mind. But after three months of careful handling, three months of tender loving care, Emma still hadn't spoken a single word since the accident that had claimed her mother's life.

The child psychologist he'd been consulting had told him on their last visit that a complete change of environment might be good for Emma. He'd recommended that Reeve take Emma out of the city that harbored so many memories of her mother, to somewhere peaceful and quiet, somewhere where she could begin to heal emotionally.

Although he'd already sent his father his regrets that he wouldn't be attending the wedding due for the most part to Emma's condition, when he'd spotted the invitation sitting atop a pile of files on his desk, he'd suddenly felt sure that Stuart's Cove, the sleepy little resort town on the west coast of

Vancouver Island where he'd spent his own happy childhood, was exactly what the doctor had prescribed.

Besides, if the truth be known, he was in need of a change of scenery himself. For the past three months, he'd been watching and waiting, hoping and praying for a break-through, something that would tell him the healing process had begun and that Emma was ready to emerge from the silent world she'd chosen.

Perhaps here, in Stuart's Cove, he would find the key to unlock the pain that was eating her up inside. Perhaps here, the emotional barriers Emma had erected would finally crumble. Perhaps here, they could find each other again.

★　★　★

In the kitchen, Shay added a decorative sprig of parsley to the last few plates of tarragon chicken with homemade cole-slaw, sweet baby carrots and tiny new potatoes waiting to be served.

She glanced up as Cheryl, one of three high school girls she'd hired as servers, appeared through the swing doors.

'We're short two place settings at the head table,' Cheryl said as she set down an empty tray.

Shay immediately realized that the two missing settings were undoubtedly for Reeve and Emma. Intent on keeping thoughts of Reeve at bay, she hadn't considered the fact that his unexpected appearance might affect the numbers.

'I'll take care of it,' she said. 'Clear away the salad plates, then take these entrées out. They're all ready to go.' She nodded toward the tray of plates she'd been working on.

Picking up two place settings wrapped in pink linen napkins, Shay headed out of the kitchen and into the area where the tables had been set up for the wedding guests. She'd spent most of the morning getting every-thing ready for the reception. The ten tables spread around the room were adorned with pink tablecloths that matched the napkins in Shay's hand. On each table stood a bud vase with a single red rose and a spray of baby's breath.

As Shay wound her way toward the head table, she passed by Mandy seated with Reverend Hardcastle and flashed her daughter a brief smile.

'Mommy, where are you going?' Mandy asked as she hopped down from her chair and began to follow her mother.

Shay stopped and turned to her daughter. 'I'm working, darling. Remember?' she said. 'Go back to your seat. I'll see you later.'

'Can't I help?' Mandy asked.

'You can help by going back to your seat,' said Shay patiently. 'Wait here. I'll be right back,' Shay said, before continuing on her way.

Mandy ignored her mother's request and followed her to the head table.

'I brought two extra settings,' Shay said, putting the items down in front of

Reeve and Emma.

Reeve smiled. 'Thank you. Oh . . . hello,' he went on, his glance sliding past Shay. 'You must be Mandy,' he said, sending Shay's heart kicking against her breast in wild panic.

'Yes, I am,' Mandy replied. 'Who are you?'

'Mandy, don't be impolite.' Shay chastised her daughter. 'Let's get you back to your seat,' she said, determined to put some distance between Mandy and the man who was her father.

'It's so boring there,' Mandy complained. 'Nobody talks to me.'

'Perhaps you'd like to sit with Emma, instead?' Alice suggested.

'No!' The word exploded from Shay, and immediately she felt her face grow hot with embarrassment when she realized that everyone at the head table, including Emma, was staring at her. 'It's just that . . . I mean . . . well, there's no room,' she blustered, wishing the floor would open up and swallow her. 'Mandy's just fine where she is.'

'But, Mom, there aren't any other kids to sit with,' Mandy wailed. 'Can't I sit with Emma?' Her blue eyes regarded Shay with bewilderment.

For the second time in as many minutes, Shay felt as if she'd been thrust into the limelight and asked to perform without a safety net. Aware of Reeve's puzzled gaze on her, she wondered if he could see, or perhaps sense, the feeling of apprehension coursing through her.

'She's more than welcome to sit with Emma.' Reeve's deep resonant voice cut through the silence.

Shay lifted her eyes to meet his, and as their glances collided, the protest hovering on her lips evaporated. To object further would simply arouse his curiosity. She dropped her gaze. 'If you're sure it's all right. Thank you,' Shay said, accepting defeat with tight-lipped politeness.

'Thanks, Mom.' Mandy's dimple appeared as she grinned at her mother. Scurrying around the table, she jumped onto the empty seat next to Emma.

'I'd better get back to the kitchen,' Shay said. Without waiting for a reply, she made her escape, silently assuring herself she had nothing to worry about, that even though Mandy tended to chatter, there was nothing the child could say that would alert Reeve to the fact that she was his daughter.

For the next hour, Shay didn't have time to think about anything except the business at hand. When the girls left with the last of the dessert trays laden with fresh strawberries and whipped cream, Shay began to relax. Everything appeared to have gone smoothly, and most of the comments her helpers had overheard and relayed to her had been positive.

With a sigh, she turned back to the sink and began to rinse more dishes. The noise of running water drowned out the sound of the door being opened behind her.

'So this is where you're hiding,' Reeve said in a teasing tone.

Shay gasped and spun around, startled by his unexpected appearance which sent her heart into a tailspin. 'Is there something I can get for you?' Shay asked, relieved that her voice sounded normal while her pulse beat out an erratic rhythm.

'No. Thank you,' he replied. 'The meal, by the way, was delicious.'

'Thank you.' Shay reached for a towel to dry her hands, warmed by the compliment.

'Alice tells me you're a chef. That you trained in France,' he went on.

'Yes,' Shay answered cautiously.

'So that's why you ran off to Europe without a word,' Reeve commented.

Alarm and another emotion not readily definable shivered its way down Shay's spine. 'That's right,' she said evenly. But it was only half of the truth. She hadn't enrolled in the cooking school her aunt and a friend started until three months after Amanda was born.

'Really? You didn't say anything that

night . . . ' Reeve's voice trailed off into silence, a silence that was suddenly crackling with tension as the memory of the last time they'd seen each other reared up between them.

'No, I didn't say anything,' Shay responded, all the while willing herself to remain calm, to maintain an air of nonchalance she was far from feeling.

Reeve held her gaze for a long moment then shrugged his shoulders. 'I came to ask for a favor,' he said at last.

'A favor?'

'My father just told me that he and Alice have arranged to have some renovations done to the house while they're on their honeymoon. They started work on it today.'

'Oh . . . that's right,' Shay said, recalling the couple's plans to modernize the kitchen and add an ensuite bathroom to the master bedroom.

'It's my own fault, of course,' Reeve went on. 'I should have called and told my father we were coming, but I assumed that even though they'd be

31

leaving for a honeymoon, Emma and I could stay at the house. But that's out of the question.'

'I see,' Shay said, still confused as to what she could do to help.

'Alice mentioned that you are almost ready to open up your bed-and-breakfast inn,' Reeve said. 'I was wondering if you could see your way to renting Emma and me a couple of rooms?'

2

Reeve's request sent shock waves through Shay, and for a moment she couldn't respond.

Suddenly, the door behind Reeve opened, and Shay swayed a little in relief when his gray eyes left hers to turn to the newcomer.

'Oh . . . I'm sorry,' Cheryl said, coming to a halt.

'No problem,' Reeve assured her with a smile.

Cheryl blinked in response to the smile and turned reluctantly to Shay. 'Ah . . . Ms. O'Brien, we've finished clearing away the dessert plates,' Cheryl said. 'Is it all right if we take a fifteen-minute break?'

'Of course,' Shay replied, glad for the distraction that allowed her the time she needed to regain her composure.

'Thanks,' Cheryl said. 'We'll be

outside if you need us,' she added before backing out of the kitchen.

'Those girls did a good job,' Reeve said, turning to Shay.

'Yes, they did,' Shay answered, feeling in control once again. It was obvious from the way Reeve was looking at her that he was still waiting for her response to his question. The idea of having Reeve and Emma staying at the inn was not Shay's idea of fun. But how could she refuse?

Reeve watched the array of emotions flit across Shay's features and wondered at the flash of fear he'd seen in the depths of her pale blue eyes. He knew he was imposing on their old friendship by asking, but after his father and Alice had explained about the renovations they were having done, Alice had been the one who'd suggested the inn as a viable alternative, saying she doubted Shay would turn away business.

But Shay didn't appear to be jumping up and down with enthusiasm at the idea of having a paying customer. Reeve frowned.

'Listen, if it's not convenient, just say so. I'll certainly understand,' He watched as Shay's cheeks turned pink.

'No, really, it's not that,' Shay said, knowing Reeve had sensed her unwillingness to comply. 'I . . . you surprised me, that's all.' Her excuse was weak and she knew it, but she held his gaze, daring him to challenge her. 'You and Emma are welcome to stay at the inn, as my guests, of course.'

'Thank you, Shay,' Reeve returned politely. 'But I can't let you do that. Hasn't anybody told you that giving freebies to friends isn't a good way to conduct business?' Though his tone held a teasing quality, Shay knew by the glint in his eyes that he was serious, and that there was little point in arguing.

Besides, he was right, she really couldn't afford not to charge him the going rate, not with a loan payment due in another month. It had taken all of her savings and more to upgrade her aunt's kitchen, put in a new water heater, give the bedrooms a fresh coat of paint and to generally put the inn back in order.

'Fine.' Shay managed a smile. 'We can sort it out later. You'll have to excuse me. It's time for your father and Alice to cut the wedding cake.'

'I'll see you back at the inn, then,' Reeve said before turning and disappearing through the swing doors.

Shay leaned against the sink and stared at the spot where Reeve had been standing, telling herself that there was no reason for her to feel in the least threatened by the prospect of having him and Emma spend a day or two at the inn.

The fact that Charles and Alice were leaving later that evening for a three-week honeymoon made the probability of Reeve and his daughter staying until their return highly unlikely. With this thought firmly planted in the forefront of her mind, Shay felt marginally better as she wheeled the trolley with the three-tiered wedding cake into the reception hall.

* * *

An hour and a half later with the help of the students, Shay had loaded up the station wagon with the boxes of dishes and glasses she'd rented for the reception. Once or twice during her forays into the hall to collect the last few coffee cups, Shay had noticed Mandy still sitting with Emma at the head table.

It wasn't until after the three student helpers had gone home that Shay, giving the kitchen a final inspection, realized Mandy had been uncharacteristically quiet since she'd come running into the kitchen fifteen minutes ago.

'Did you have a good time today, darling?' Shay asked, coming to a halt beside her daughter who was sitting on a stool at the counter.

'Yes. It was fun.'

'Well, everything appears to be back

the way we found it,' Shay announced, scanning the room one last time to see if she had forgotten anything. 'Let's go home.'

Mandy hopped down from the stool and ran out the rear exit to the car parked outside.

Though most of the guests had already gone, Shay noticed the group of people gathered around Alice and Charles on the grassy verge in front of the hall. She had no trouble picking out Reeve, his six-foot-two-inch frame easily recognizable amid the small crowd. Beside him stood Emma, still clutching the rag doll. Shay couldn't help noticing that his daughter looked tired and pale.

'Buckle up,' Shay said. Flashing Mandy a smile, she started the engine. Shay was suddenly aware of the silence in the car, an unusual phenomenon whenever Mandy was around.

'Did you have fun with Emma? What did the two of you talk about?' Shay asked, thinking that this would be all the encouragement Mandy would need to launch into a minute-by-minute account of their conversation.

'Nothing much,' Mandy answered.

Shay threw her daughter a surprised glance. 'Nothing much? Emma's a bit shy, then.'

'No,' came the reply. 'She just doesn't talk,' Mandy said.

'Do you mean she can't talk?' Shay frowned, beginning to feel like a detective interviewing an uncooperative witness.

'Her daddy told me she can talk,' Mandy replied. 'But she just doesn't like to anymore.'

'Does she have a cold or laryngitis or something?' Shay asked.

'No, Mom.' Mandy sighed with exasperation. 'She doesn't like to talk anymore, that's all,' she explained.

Shay was silent as they left the outskirts of Stuart's Cove and turned onto Beach Road, which ran parallel to the ocean. The eight-bedroom bed-and-breakfast inn that had once belonged to her aunt was located at the far end of Beach Road. Several other older homes, including the house belonging to Reeve's father and each with an outstanding view of the ocean, were spread out behind them on higher ground. Below the inn a paved pathway led to the small, sandy cove that adjoined the larger cove named for the town.

As she drove the remaining distance to the inn, Shay was still trying to make sense of what Mandy had told her about Emma.

'What did you talk to Emma about?' Shay asked.

'I just told her all about myself,' Mandy replied. 'I told her that we came to live here a few months ago, and that I like it a lot, especially being able to play on the beach. And I told her that I want to be a doctor when I grew up, and I told her about the kitten I found — '

'I get the idea,' Shay interrupted with a laugh, wondering what Emma thought as she was being bombarded with the information.

'Did her father say why she doesn't talk? Has she been ill, or was she in an accident or something?' Shay asked as she turned into the driveway leading to the rear entrance of the inn.

'I don't know, Mom' came the reply. 'He just said he's sure Emma will talk again one day soon.' Mandy let out a heartfelt sigh. 'I sure wish I could help Emma. She looks so sad.'

Shay glanced at her daughter and felt a rush of love for her. Ever since Mandy was quite small, she'd been a sensitive and caring child, and Shay was convinced that Mandy already had many of the qualities needed to become an outstanding physician.

'Mandy, could you help me carry the cooler inside?' Shay said as she brought the car to a halt.

'I want to take off this dress first,' Mandy said. 'And we should check on Patches,' Mandy said, referring to the eight-week-old stray calico kitten she'd

41

found wandering on the dunes only last week. 'She's been shut up in the kitchen since lunchtime.'

'Oh . . . right,' Shay replied. They hadn't wanted to let the kitten roam free outside, but gave her the run of the kitchen instead.

Leaving the cooler for the moment, Shay caught up with Mandy and unlocked the back door. Mandy was inside in a flash and, without regard to her pink dress, dropped onto her hands and knees beside the cardboard box lined with an old blanket, where the kitten lay sleeping.

'She's eaten all the food we left, and there's only a little milk left in the bowl,' Mandy reported.

Shay smiled as she watched the tiny kitten stretch before jumping out of its makeshift bed. Glancing at the litter box nearby, she noted with a sigh that most of its contents were scattered over the floor. As she continued to survey the room, she noticed that the small vase of flowers on the table had been knocked over, and water was dripping onto the white linen runner that lay in a crumpled heap on the floor.

'It's amazing what a little kitten can do in only a few hours,' she commented as she gazed at the mess.

'Aw . . . Mom!' Mandy said, gathering the kitten into her arms, where it happily snuggled against her throat and began to purr loudly. 'Nothing's broken. And I promise I'll clean it all up.'

'All right,' Shay said. When Mandy first brought the stray kitten home, she had tried to take a firm stand with her daughter, explaining to her that pets were a big responsibility. But Mandy had begged and pleaded to keep the kitten, promising she'd take care of it all.

Shay hadn't had the heart to refuse. How could she, when at the time, the rather bedraggled, orange, black and white bundle had been purring contentedly in her arms?

'Go and change out of your dress,' Shay said.

'I'll take Patches with me. That way, she won't get into any more trouble,' Mandy said, already halfway to her room at the front of the house.

Tempted though she was to get the mop and broom and begin cleaning up, Shay set down her purse and slowly made her way outside. As she opened the rear door of the wagon, another vehicle pulled into the driveway.

Glancing around, a flurry of emotion rippled through her. She drew a steadying breath and pinned a smile on her face. 'I didn't expect you so soon,' she said as Reeve brought the car to a halt next to the wagon.

'My father and Alice went to check in their luggage at the airport. They were meeting Dr. Billings there, too,' he said. 'She's the doctor Dad hired to look after things here while he and Alice are on their honeymoon. She's flying in from Vancouver.'

'Right.' Alice had mentioned something about a doctor coming from Vancouver to look after Charles's small medical clinic while they were away.

'The inn looks great,' Reeve said as he uncoiled his long, lean body from the driver's seat. 'That new coat of paint certainly does wonders for the place,' he commented as he came around to open the passenger door for Emma.

'Thank you,' Shay replied. When she'd first arrived at the inn, the paint had been weathered and peeling, and the shrubbery had been badly over-grown.

Instead of trying to tackle it all herself, she'd hired students to paint the outside of the house and clean up the garden. She'd repainted the bedrooms, and in just two short months her aunt's bed-and-breakfast inn had been transformed into the picturesque place she remembered as a child. Though she'd had to take out a loan to cover the cost of upgrading the kitchen, she'd told herself it was well worth it to see the inn looking like its old self again.

'Can Emma and I give you a hand with anything?' Reeve asked, cutting into Shay's thoughts.

'I just need to bring in the cooler. I rented the dishes and glasses from a place in town,' Shay said. 'I'll leave those in the wagon and take them back on Monday. Hello, Emma,' she said, smiling at the child, who was standing close to her father. 'Did you have a good time at the wedding?'

Emma shuffled closer to her father and, clutching her rag doll tightly against her breast, stared down at her shoes.

'Mommy, I heard a car — ' Mandy, wearing blue shorts and white T-shirt, came barreling out of the house, braking to a halt when she caught sight of Emma and her father. 'Emma! What are you doing here?'

'Mandy, mind your manners,' Shay scolded. 'Emma and Ree . . . her father will be staying at the inn for a few days.'

'They will?' Mandy's eyes sparkled with excitement. 'Neato! Want to come and see Patches, my kitten? I told you about her, remember? She made a mess in the kitchen when we were out, and I have to clean it up. But that won't take long, then we can play with her if you like,' Mandy continued as she came toward them.

Emma's chin lifted a little. From beneath her long lashes, she peeked at Mandy. For a split second, Shay saw a glimmer of interest in the depths of the child's eyes.

Reeve saw it, too, and felt his pulse quicken. This was the first time he'd glimpsed anything even resembling emotion in his daughter's eyes. 'Sweetheart, would you like to play with Mandy and her kitten?' he asked, praying she would voice her response.

But at her father's question, Emma lowered her head once more, sending a wave of disappointment crashing over Reeve. He'd thought she was about to make a breakthrough, but as his hopes plummeted he wondered if perhaps he'd only imagined the spark of interest he'd seen in her eyes.

'Is it all right if I take Emma inside with me?' Mandy asked, oblivious to the tension shimmering in the air between Emma and her father.

'Of course,' Reeve replied, all the while thinking that Mandy appeared to be one of the few people who seemed to be taking Emma's unwillingness to speak in stride.

Mandy grinned at Emma. 'Come on,' she said. Taking Emma's hand she began to lead her toward the house. 'You're going to love it here. I'll show you all my favorite places . . . '

Reeve stood gazing after the children, telling himself he'd been foolish to get his hopes up. But after three months of silence, he would be willing to sell his soul to the devil if he could just see his daughter smile or hear her voice again.

'You can tell me it's none of my business, if you like,' Shay said once the children had disappeared inside. 'What's wrong with Emma? Why doesn't she talk?'

Reeve was silent for so long Shay wondered if he'd even heard her question. She'd seen the flare of hope in Reeve's eyes as he watched his daughter, and she'd been achingly aware of his disappointment when Emma had made no verbal response.

Shay could still see the tension in every line of his body, and she was almost tempted to reach out and comfort him, to soothe away the worry etched on his handsome features.

But that wasn't a job for her. That was a job for his wife. Where was his wife? The question slammed into Shay's mind, squashing her original impulse. Why wasn't Louise here to care for her daughter and comfort her husband?

'There's nothing wrong, at least nothing physical,' Reeve said at last. 'The specialist has assured me Emma will speak again, one day,' he added, but Shay heard the doubt echoing in his voice.

'Shouldn't her mother be with her?' Shay blurted out the question that had been hovering at the forefront of her mind, at a loss to understand why Emma's mother was absent, especially when her daughter so obviously needed her.

Reeve was gazing at her as if she'd suddenly grown a set of antlers. His eyes seemed to glaze over, and his features contorted briefly into an expression of anger and anguish, telling her clearly that she'd hit a raw nerve.

'Emma's mother is dead.' Reeve's expression was bleak, his voice devoid of emotion.

Shay stared in stunned silence at the man before her. 'Oh . . . God . . . I'm so sorry,' she managed to mutter, reeling from the shock of his announcement. 'I had no idea,' she added, knowing that no matter what she said, her words would be totally inadequate, yet she wanted to at least try to atone for her blunder.

'Louise was killed in a car accident three months ago,' Reeve went on almost as if he hadn't heard her. 'Emma was a passenger in the vehicle and escaped with only a few scratches. She hasn't spoken a word since.'

Shay heard the desolation in his tone and for the second time in as many minutes, she was overwhelmed with the need to comfort him. 'Oh, Reeve . . . how awful for you,' she said, reaching out to take his hand in hers.

At the contact, a ripple of sensation scurried up Shay's arm but she ignored it, intent only on wanting to console him.

Reeve felt a shudder vibrate through him as Shay's hand curled comfortingly around his. He could feel her compassion and her warmth slowly seeping into him. Somehow, the gesture stole through his defenses to soften the hard nugget of guilt he'd been carrying around for so long, guilt brought on by the fact that he blamed himself for Emma's having been with her mother on the night of the accident.

Emma had been spending the week-end with him, a rare concession given by his ex-wife. But it had come as no surprise when Louise had shown up at his apartment late that Saturday afternoon on some pretext he couldn't even recall, saying she'd come to take Emma home.

Emma hadn't wanted to go, which had angered Louise, and as a result she'd lashed out at him, accusing him of turning her daughter against her. He'd refused to fight with Louise in front of Emma, feeling that the child had been put through enough since the divorce. But as he'd helped Emma gather her toys and pack her things, he'd vowed to battle the courts and fight for custody of his daughter once more. He'd felt as if his heart was being torn from his chest as he watched Emma, her face stained with tears, leave with her mother.

Each day, Reeve thanked the powers that be for the fact that Emma had survived the accident. But he wasn't sure he'd ever be able to forgive himself if she didn't recover fully from the emotional wounds inflicted on her as a result of the ordeal.

'She's too damned young to be dealing with something like this.' Reeve's voice was little more than a whisper.

'Children are remarkably resilient creatures,' Shay said quietly. 'I'm sure she'll come out of it. All you have to do is love her, be patient and give her time.' She knew her words were merely platitudes, but she had to say them.

Reeve heard the genuine concern in Shay's voice and felt the knot of tension inside him begin to ease. 'Do you know something? I believe you,' he said and gently squeezed her hand with his. 'Several of my colleagues, as well as Emma's specialist, have all been telling me the same thing for the past three months, but I could never quite bring myself to believe any of them.' He stopped and gazed deeply into her eyes. 'But I believe *you*. Why is that, do you suppose?' he asked, a smile tugging playfully at the corners of his mouth.

Shay felt a tremor race through her. His smile was doing strange things to her pulse; her lungs seemed to have forgotten how to function, and she wasn't altogether sure just how she'd come to be standing so close to him, their bodies almost touching, their breaths mingling, their fingers slowly entwining in a loverlike grasp.

But she was a willing prisoner, mesmerized by the look she could see in the depths of his gray eyes, a look that had her spinning back in time to a summer's night so long ago, a night she would never forget.

He was going to kiss her, she was sure of it and for the life of her she couldn't move as she waited in breathless anticipation for his mouth to claim hers.

'Thanks,' she heard Reeve say, breaking the spell, and leaving her to combat the sudden rush of disappointment reverberating through her. 'I'd better check on Emma,' he went on, taking a step away from her. 'She looked a little tired, and she didn't sleep much on the flight from New York,' he said. 'Did you say you needed help with something?' he added, moving to the rear of the station wagon.

'Ah, yes . . . if you could bring the cooler inside,' Shay told him, feeling a blush slowly stain her cheeks.

As Reeve lifted the cooler from the wagon, Shay crossed to the kitchen door and held it open. Once inside, Shay was pleased to note that Mandy had followed through on her promise to clean up the kitten's mess.

Shay could hear the sound of Mandy's voice coming from her bedroom. When they'd moved into the house, Shay had asked Mandy which bedroom she would like, only to have her daughter request the room Shay had occupied when she'd first moved to Stuart's Cove at the age of ten, to live with her aunt Isabel.

Shay had opted for her aunt's bedroom, which was right next door to Mandy's, for the simple reason that it was the only bedroom with its own private bathroom. Upstairs on the second floor, there were three bedrooms and a bathroom, and three more bedrooms and a bathroom on the third floor.

While the house also had a full basement, that area was unfinished and used mainly for storage purposes. During the time her aunt had been running the bed-and-breakfast inn, she'd had a small wine cellar built, but at the moment there were only a dozen or so bottles of wine remaining on the shelves.

With plans to expand her venture and offer evening meals to her guests as well as the standard breakfast, Shay hoped to restock the cellar and have on hand a variety of fine wines to tempt the most discerning palate.

'The children are down the hall in Mandy's bedroom,' Shay said, closing the kitchen door. 'Do you want me to call them?' she asked as Reeve set the cooler on the kitchen table.

'There's no rush,' Reeve replied. 'If you show me which of your rooms we can use, I'll bring in our luggage first.'

'Fine,' Shay said. 'Follow me.'

Shay led the way through the large dining room across the brightly lit entrance, to the staircase leading to the second floor. At the top of the stairs, she turned right, coming to a halt at the door of the largest of the three bedrooms.

'The bathroom is directly opposite,' she told him as she opened the bedroom door. Shay held her breath as Reeve brushed past her into the spacious room furnished with a double bed, an antique oak dressing table and matching wardrobe and a night table with a brass reading lamp.

Reeve quickly scanned the room. 'This is great.'

'Emma can stay in the room next door.' Shay crossed to the adjoining door and unlocked it.

Reeve followed and, drawing level with her, he glanced inside the other room. 'She'll love it,' he said, flashing Shay a smile.

Shay's breath caught in her throat. Suddenly, the bedroom seemed small and intimate, due no doubt to Reeve's proximity. Gamely, she tried to ignore the sensations coursing through her.

'Do you know I don't remember ever seeing any of the rooms in this house before, other than the kitchen,' he said as he turned to her. 'The No Vacancy sign always seemed to be hanging up outside. Your aunt had quite a little gold mine going here. I never understood why she closed up the place, or why the two of you flew off to Europe and stayed away so long.'

A shiver of alarm sped along Shay's nerve endings at Reeve's comments, but she kept her expression neutral as she headed toward the door.

'Why *did* you stay away so long?' he asked.

Shay moistened lips that were dry. 'Aunt Isabel spent a year in France after she got out of college. She'd made quite a few friends there,' Shay answered carefully. 'We paid them a visit, and while we were in Provence, one of her friends invited Aunt Izzy to go into business with her,' she explained as they retraced their steps to the kitchen.

'Is that where you met Mandy's father?' Reeve asked casually.

Shay felt her breath lock in her throat and her heart kick wildly against her rib cage in response to his question. She couldn't think of an answer, and when Mandy and Emma suddenly appeared, Shay sent up a silent prayer of thanks for the timely interruption.

Emma ran up to her father and held out the kitten to him.

'Emma thinks Patches is really cute, and she'd like a kitten of her own one day,' Mandy said, crossing to the refrigerator.

Reeve's glance darted to Mandy then to Emma. 'Did you say that, sweetheart?' he asked his daughter, a faint thread of hope in his voice.

'She didn't have to,' Mandy responded. 'I can tell what Emma's thinking just by looking into her eyes. They're the exact color as mine, you know,' she added, tossing that little gem of information at them moments before her brown curls disappeared behind the open fridge door.

Shay glanced at Reeve to see if Mandy's comments had made any impact, and she almost sagged with relief that he appeared totally absorbed in watching his daughter stroke the kitten. Patches began to wriggle in Emma's arms.

'I think the kitten wants to get down.' Reeve gently lifted Patches out of his daughter's hands.

Once on the floor, the kitten made a beeline for its food dishes, only to start meowing when she discovered they were empty.

'Patches only meows like that when she's hungry,' Mandy said as she withdrew a carton of milk from the fridge. 'Want to help me feed her?' she asked Emma. 'I'll pour some milk first, then I'll show you where we keep the dry food. It's in the pantry.'

Emma moved to where Mandy was crouching beside the kitten. After returning the milk, Mandy took Emma's hand and led her to the walk-in pantry on the other side of the kitchen.

'Good heavens!' Reeve suddenly exclaimed. 'It's amazing. I can't believe it.'

Shay spun around to look at him. She could see by the excitement glittering in the depths of his steely gray eyes that something significant had happened. But what? Had he seen the faint resemblance between the two girls? Had he somehow guessed the truth about Mandy?

3

'What is it? What's wrong?' Shay asked, though she wasn't altogether sure she wanted to hear Reeve's answer.

'Nothing's wrong,' he replied. 'In fact, it's wonderful.' His smile widened.

'Wonderful?' Shay repeated, feeling her pulse kick into high gear in reaction to his smile.

'I just noticed — ' He broke off abruptly as Mandy and Emma emerged from the pantry, carrying a five-pound bag of kitten food between them. 'Hey! That looks heavy. Need any help?' Reeve asked.

Mandy flashed him a smile, exposing her dimple. 'Thanks, but Emma and me can manage,' she assured him.

Shay noted a look of puzzlement that flitted across Reeve's forehead and wondered at the reason for it. But more important, she wondered just what he'd been so excited about a few moments ago. Whatever it was had to do with Emma and Mandy or both. The thought sent a shiver of apprehension through her.

'I'll hold the bag open,' Mandy was saying. 'If you look inside, you'll find a plastic cup. Just scoop some food out and put it in Patches's bowl. She'll be there in a jiffy.'

Shay watched as Emma carefully followed the instructions. As Mandy had predicted, the moment the dry kitten chow landed in the second bowl, Patches abandoned the milk she'd been drinking and scampered toward Emma, immediately giving her full attention to the food supply.

'See, I told you.' Mandy beamed with pleasure and Shay saw Emma's mouth curve fleetingly in what might have been the beginning of a smile.

'You don't have to haul the bag out each time, sweetie,' Shay told her daughter. 'All you need to do is scoop some into the cup and bring it out,' she added when Mandy reappeared.

'We'll do that next time,' Mandy replied easily. 'Is it all right if we watch TV in the living room for a while?'

Shay glanced at Reeve, who met her silent query with a brief nod. 'Sure, but only for half an hour,' she cautioned. 'It will be bedtime soon, and you still have to finish tidying your room. You didn't have time this morning, remember?'

'But my room isn't untidy,' Mandy protested.

'That's a matter of opinion,' Shay responded dryly.

'Can we each have an apple while we watch TV?' Mandy asked, ignoring her mother's comment.

'*May* we,' Shay automatically corrected. 'And yes, there's a bowl of apples on the dining room table. Help yourselves.'

'Come on, Emma,' Mandy said and, with that, the twosome made their way from the kitchen.

'I still can't believe it,' Reeve said once the children had left. 'But one thing is certain, it's the breakthrough I've been praying for.'

'Breakthrough?' Shay repeated with a frown. 'I'm not sure I understand.'

Reeve turned to face her. 'Ever since the accident, Emma has never been without her rag doll, Susie,' he said. 'She carries it with her everywhere, never lets it out of her sight, only relinquishing it with great reluctance when she takes a bath.'

Shay suddenly saw the significance. 'Emma wasn't carrying Susie,' she stated.

'Exactly,' Reeve cut in as he came to a halt in front of her. 'It may not seem like much, but as far as I'm concerned, it's very meaningful and definitely an encouraging sign.'

'I think you're right,' Shay said softly.

'Thank you,' Reeve said, his tone heartfelt. He hadn't realized just how much he'd needed to hear those words of support. For the past three months, he'd been fighting a solitary battle against enemies he couldn't even see.

Feelings of despair and frustration had often threatened to overwhelm him and throughout it all, he'd had no one with whom to share the burden, no one to talk to or to help ease the pain and guilt weighing heavily on his shoulders.

'You deserve some credit, too, you know — ' Reeve went on, cheerfulness still evident in his tone.

Shay stared at him in bewilderment. 'Me? What did I do?'

'Well, you're Mandy's mother, and she's the one I should really be thanking. She's the one who's keeping Emma busy, too busy to think or worry about Susie,' Reeve explained. 'It's obvious Mandy has appointed herself Emma's friend and protector. A big sister, you might say,' he added with a smile.

Shay felt her heart shudder in her breast at his comment, and she found herself wondering just what his reaction would be if he knew how close to the truth he really was.

A knock at the kitchen door distracted their attention. With a sharp sense of relief, Shay crossed to open it.

'Alice. Dr. Walker.' Shay greeted the couple standing in the doorway. 'I didn't hear a car. Please, come in. Is everything all right?' she asked, noting that Alice looked more than a little downcast.

'Hello! Aren't you supposed to be catching a plane?' Reeve asked.

'The flight doesn't leave for another hour,' Charles told them. 'But I'm afraid we're going to have to miss it,' he said disappointedly.

'Miss it? But why? What happened? You're not ill, are you?' Reeve countered, concern in his voice.

'No, it's nothing like that,' Charles quickly assured his son.

'Dr. Billings wasn't on the flight from Vancouver,' Alice explained.

'Dr. Billings?' Reeve frowned. 'Oh . . . the doctor who was going to take care of your clinic while the two of you go on your honeymoon.'

'Right.' His father replied.

'She didn't arrive?' Reeve queried. 'Maybe she just missed the flight and is coming in on a later one.'

Charles shook his head. 'I wish that was the case,' he responded with a sigh. 'Unfortunately, it's more serious than that.'

'When Dr. Billings didn't appear, your father called her in Vancouver,' Alice took up the story. 'Denise has been living with her parents since she got back from Africa where she'd been working with the Red Cross. Her mother answered the phone.' Alice paused. 'The long and short of it is, Dr. Billings was admitted to hospital this afternoon with a badly broken ankle after falling down their basement stairs.'

'Oh, no! How awful,' Shay said.

'As a result, she'll be a patient herself for a while and won't be flying anywhere,' Charles concluded the tale.

'And it's rather late to even try and find someone to replace her,' Alice said, smiling bravely in spite of her obvious disappointment.

'Thank goodness I took out cancellation insurance on the trip,' Charles said, putting his arm around his wife's shoulders and dropping a kiss on her temple. 'We'll just have to see Paris another time, darling.'

'We can go next year, when you retire,' Alice said, smiling up at him. 'Although I've heard you say that finding a doctor willing to leave the big city and take over a small clinic won't be easy then, either.'

'Oh . . . the renovations . . . I almost forgot,' Charles said. 'We'll have to call the workmen from Blyth Construction in the morning. I just hope they haven't made too much of a mess already.'

'Dad? Did you cancel your flight yet?' Reeve cut in, a hint of urgency in his tone.

'No. We hadn't even checked in. After I talked to Denise's mother, well, we didn't see the point, so we turned around and drove here,' his father said. 'Why?'

'Because you don't have to cancel anything. You're going to Paris. That's why,' Reeve declared decisively.

'But how can we?' Alice asked, gazing at her stepson in bewilderment.

'Because I say so,' Reeve countered with a smile. 'What time does the flight to Vancouver leave?'

Charles glanced at his wristwatch. 'In forty-five minutes, but — '

'No buts, Dad,' Reeve interrupted. 'You haven't taken a holiday in years, and I know how much you've both been looking forward to this trip. I'll take care of everything at the clinic till you get back. I *am* a doctor, remember?' He flashed his father a grin. 'It's my wedding gift to you both. And as for the renovations, well, they can go on as planned, too. Emma and I can stay here at the inn. That's not a problem, is it, Shay?' Reeve turned to Shay who'd been silent throughout his startling discourse.

Shay moistened lips that were suddenly dry. 'A problem?' she repeated.

'Well, I'm not ... that is ... '
Suddenly, she was aware of three pairs of eyes anxiously awaiting her reply. 'There's no problem whatsoever,' she concluded brightly, ignoring the tiny voice inside her head telling her she was a fool.

Having Reeve Walker and his daughter living under the same roof for three weeks would be a hardship indeed, but she couldn't bring herself to dim the glimmer of hope she'd seen in Alice's eyes.

'That's settled then,' Reeve said.

'But are you sure, son?' Charles asked, still sounding skeptical. 'What about your job in New York? Don't you have to be back?'

'Not for at least three weeks,' Reeve said smoothly. 'Listen, Dad, you don't have time to argue,' he told him. 'Not if you want to make that flight.'

Charles grasped Reeve by the shoulders and subjected him to a bear hug. 'Thanks, son. I owe you one,' he said as he withdrew.

'Reeve, I don't know how to thank you,' Alice said, hugging him.

'You just did,' Reeve said easily. 'Now, you'd better get out of here before I change my mind,' he teased.

'You'll need these,' Charles said as he pulled a set of keys from his pocket. 'They're an extra set of keys to the clinic,' Charles added. 'Brenda Hoover, my head nurse, will be able to fill you in on how things are run. Oh, and — '

'Don't worry, Dad. I'll figure it all out,' Reeve assured him.

Alice's eyes were brimming with tears of happiness. She smiled her thanks to Shay, then, taking her husband's hand, they headed for the door.

'Have fun, and don't worry about a thing,' Reeve ordered as he stood with Shay in the doorway and watched Alice and his father hurry toward their car.

'Have a wonderful time,' Shay called out as Charles drove the car out of the driveway. With a final wave, they were off.

Reeve turned to Shay and smiled.

'Thanks,' he said.

'For what?' she asked as she closed the door.

'For backing me up,' he replied. 'You don't mind if Emma and I stay here for the duration, do you?'

Shay crossed to the sink and turned on the water. 'Why would I mind?' she countered, a hint of annoyance leaking into her tone. She did mind — she minded very much — but overriding her misgivings was the fact that she couldn't in good conscience turn away a paying customer, and certainly not one proposing to stay for three weeks.

'Beats me,' Reeve said. Though he couldn't quite put his finger on it, he knew something was bothering her. He could tell by the edge in her voice and the way her eyes looked away from his. All at once, he remembered the flicker of panic he'd seen in their depths a few moments ago when he'd asked her if he and Emma could stay.

'Then there's no problem?' Reeve

didn't quite know why he was persisting, but as he watched the color rising in Shay's cheeks, he knew his instincts were right. Before he could continue, Mandy and Emma appeared.

'Is Patches in here?' Mandy asked.

'I don't know,' Shay replied, setting the plate she'd been rinsing onto the draining board. 'Isn't she asleep in her cardboard box?'

'No,' came her daughter's reply. 'You didn't let her outside, did you, Mom?' Mandy asked, a hint of anxiety in her voice.

'No . . . unless,' Shay began, wondering if the kitten had somehow slipped out as Dr. Walker and Alice were leaving.

'She's right here,' Reeve said, pointing to one of the cushioned kitchen chairs. 'She must have climbed up there when she finished eating.'

'Can we take her to my room?' Mandy asked.

'If she's sleeping, why don't you just leave her?' Shay suggested as she picked up a dish towel.

'No . . . she's awake, see?' Mandy said. 'I wanted to show Emma how Patches plays with the pom-pom on a string that I made for her. I told Emma I'd show her how to make one, too.'

Shay glanced at Emma in time to see the child yawn widely. 'I think it's too late to start on that tonight, Mandy,' Shay said. 'It's time to finish tidying your room and then get ready for bed.'

'Already?' Mandy groaned, pulling a face.

'I'm afraid so, darling,' Shay confirmed. 'It's nearly nine o'clock. You can show Emma how to make pom-poms tomorrow.'

Reeve crouched before his daughter. 'You look beat, sweetheart,' he said. 'It's time you were in bed.' Lifting her into his arms, he set her down on the kitchen chair nearby. 'If you wait right here, I'll bring in our suitcases.' Crossing to the back door, he slipped outside.

'Mom? Which room is Emma in?'

Mandy asked, once Reeve had gone.

'Upstairs in the blue room,' Shay replied. 'Your father is right next door, Emma,' she added, noting the worried look in the little girl's eyes.

'We call it the blue room 'cause my mom painted the walls blue,' Mandy explained. 'It's a pretty room, Emma, you'll like it. You can even see the ocean from the window.'

'All right, Mandy, time to say good-night to Emma,' Shay instructed, knowing her daughter would linger as long as possible.

''Night, Emma. See you in the morning. Sleep tight,' she added, and with a wave, she turned and slowly made her way from the room.

Moments later, the back door opened and Reeve returned, carrying two midsize suitcases and a small shoulder bag. 'Come on, poppet,' he said. 'You're almost asleep on your feet,' he teased. 'I'm feeling a bit jet lagged myself. I think we'll both turn in. Follow me and we'll soon get you settled into bed.'

Emma hopped down from the chair and made to follow her father.

'Oh . . . Emma!' Mandy reappeared in the doorway. 'You left your rag doll in my room.'

Reeve felt his heart skip a beat at the look of surprise that came and went in his daughter's eyes. His glance shifted to meet Shay's and he knew by the almost imperceptible nod that she'd seen it, too.

Taking the doll from Mandy's outstretched hands, Emma clutched it tightly to her breast before moving to where her father stood waiting.

'Thanks, Mandy,' Reeve said, flashing the child a grateful smile. 'Come on, Emma, let's put Susie to bed. I bet she's tired after her long day, too. Good night, Mandy . . . Shay,' he said as he ushered Emma from the kitchen.

''Night!' Mandy responded before skipping off to her room.

Shay stood for a moment, watching until Reeve was out of sight. The quick glance he'd thrown her way had tugged strangely at her heart.

Silently, she told herself she shouldn't get involved, that neither Emma's nor Reeve's emotional well-being were her concern. But she knew she was only fooling herself. Her friendship with Reeve went back a long way, starting from the day she'd arrived in Stuart's Cove to live with her aunt Isabel.

Shay closed her eyes for a moment as a wave of pain engulfed her. How she wished Aunt Izzy were here. How she wished she could talk to her now. Her aunt had been like a mother to her, always giving her love and support unconditionally.

When Shay had discovered she was pregnant, she'd gone immediately to her aunt and told her that she was carrying Reeve's child. Aunt Izzy had neither condemned nor judged her. She'd simply listened to Shay's faltering explanation with understanding and deep compassion. She'd supported Shay's decision to tell Reeve about the baby, but when that course of action had fallen through, Isabel had been the one who'd suggested the trip to Europe.

They'd only intended to stay until after the baby was born, but by then her aunt and several of her aunt's friends who lived in the French countryside had drawn up plans to open a cooking school. Shay had been one of their first students.

Those had been happy times. The cooking school had closed down after a successful five-year run, and Aunt Izzy had been in the middle of making plans to return to Stuart's Cove when she'd died as the result of a heart attack.

Shay had been working as a chef in a popular local restaurant at the time, but after Aunt Izzy's death, she'd suddenly found herself filled with a nostalgia and longing to come back to the place she still regarded as home.

Though she'd been shocked and dismayed at how rundown and neglected the inn had been, she'd been glad Aunt Izzy hadn't had to see it looking quite so forlorn. Not until she unlocked the door and walked inside did Shay realize how much she still loved the place, how the inn itself had somehow become a symbol for all the love and security she'd known in her life.

Some of her happiest memories were of the times she'd spent here, and Shay felt she owed it to Aunt Izzy to restore the inn to its original splendor. The cost, however, had been much more than she'd anticipated. She'd had to take out a loan at the bank, a loan she was determined to pay off as soon as possible.

And while Reeve's and Emma's presence would help in that regard, Shay knew that she needed a continuous stream of tourists from now until Thanksgiving if she had any hope of keeping up the payments on the loan.

With a sigh, Shay pushed these thoughts aside and folding the dishcloth she'd been using, locked the back door and headed down the hall to Mandy's bedroom.

Patches was curled up at the foot of Mandy's bed, fast asleep. Shay was pleased to note that Mandy had tidied her room.

'Can we read another chapter of my book?' Mandy asked, referring to the mystery story Shay had started reading to her a few nights ago.

'It's late, and I'm really tired,' Shay said, and at her words Mandy's face fell. 'Have you brushed your teeth?'

'Yes, and I even washed my face and hands, see?' her daughter replied, thrusting her hands out toward Shay for inspection.

'Good girl!' Shay said as she sat down on the edge of the bed, careful to avoid the kitten. 'You can read for a while on your own if you like.'

'Thanks, Mom,' Mandy said.

Shay leaned forward and kissed her daughter's forehead. 'Good night, sweetie.'

'Mom?' Mandy said as Shay stood up.

'Yes, dear,' Shay responded.

'Why do people get married?'

Shay's pulse skittered wildly at the question. 'Ah . . . well, because they love each other and want to spend their lives together,' she replied after a brief pause.

'Tell me again why you and my daddy didn't get married,' Mandy requested.

Shay drew a steadying breath. 'Your father and I didn't get married because he loved someone else.' That the memory still had the power to hurt surprised her, but she resolutely pushed aside the pain, having made it a rule to always answer Mandy's questions about her father as truthfully as possible.

'But you loved him, didn't you?' Mandy went on.

Shay felt her heart stumble briefly as she met her daughter's steady gaze. 'Yes, I did.'

'Will I get married one day?' Mandy wanted to know.

'Perhaps one day, when you meet the right man and fall in love.' Shay kept her tone light, feeling sure that the wedding ceremony earlier was the reason for Mandy's questions. Leaning over, Shay picked the kitten off the bed and cuddled it against her.

'But how will I know if he's the right man?' Mandy wanted to know, obviously intrigued by the subject.

Shay drew a ragged breath and fought down the emotion suddenly clogging her throat. 'Your heart will tell you,' she replied softly. 'Good night, sweetheart. Don't read too long,' she added before carrying the kitten from the room.

Returning to the kitchen, Shay sat Patches down in the animal's makeshift bed. Switching off the lights, she made her way to her own room, but once there she found she couldn't relax. She opened her bedroom window wide and, closing her eyes, listened to the waves splashing on the shore below.

Shay took several deep breaths, inhaling the tangy scent of the ocean in an attempt to soothe her troubled thoughts, but the faint noises coming from the second floor served to remind her that Reeve was indeed back in her life once more.

But then, she'd never quite been able to forget him. After all, he'd had a major influence on the path her life had taken. From the moment she'd met him, she'd looked up to him and regarded him as the brother she'd never had. And even though he was six years older, he'd accepted his role, never minding that she liked to tag along after him.

When he left Stuart's Cove to attend university on the mainland, she'd written to him every week, telling him about everything that was going on in town. And whenever he came home on long weekends or on holidays, he'd always made a point of spending time with her.

She remembered quite vividly the moment her feelings for Reeve had changed from friendship to something more, something deeper. It was Christmas Eve, Shay's eighteenth birthday and she'd been invited to a party at a friend's house in town. She'd worn a red velvet dress with a low neckline and tight skirt and was feeling sexy and a little daring when Reeve and several of his friends showed up at the party.

He'd looked incredibly attractive in a pair of dark blue jeans, a white shirt and navy blazer. He walked toward her, his mouth curving in a warm welcoming smile. As he drew nearer, his gaze skimmed over her and a look she'd never seen before had suddenly darkened his eyes.

Reeve hadn't said a word as he'd taken her hand and tugged her onto the small dance floor nearby. As his arms went around her and their bodies touched, Shay had thought she might faint, so overwhelming and earth-shattering were the sensations coursing through her.

When the song ended, he'd reluctantly drawn away and once again Shay had seen an emotion she couldn't quite decipher flicker in the depths of his gray eyes. They'd stared at each other for what seemed an eternity, then suddenly someone had thrust their way between them, and the moment was lost.

For the remainder of the evening, she'd stood in a corner waiting for Reeve to return to claim her, sure that he, too, felt what had happened between them on the dance floor. But when she'd seen him leave with his friends a little later without as much as a goodbye, she'd thought her heart would break.

Aunt Izzy's light had been on when Shay got home that night, and longing to talk to someone about those magical moments she'd shared with Reeve, she'd sat on her aunt's bed and related the story, ending with the bewilderment she'd felt when he'd left without talking to her.

Her disappointment and pain only intensified a few days later when she learned that Reeve had cut short his stay. But that didn't stop her thinking about him, or dreaming about him. She was in love with him. She was sure of it. What other explanation could there be for the emotions churning inside her?

She'd waited anxiously for Reeve's next visit home, but through the town grapevine learned that he'd planned to spend his spring-term break from university with friends in New York.

In a futile attempt to forget him, she dated several guys in her high school class. There was no magic. They weren't Reeve.

With graduation only a few months away, Shay had applied herself to her studies and even volunteered to help organize the graduation dance to be held in the high school gymnasium.

There had been times during the past ten years when she'd wondered if the outcome of that night would have been different had she known in advance that Reeve was in town visiting his father.

Somehow, she doubted it. But when he walked into the gymnasium on that hot summer's night, she'd thought she was dreaming. She'd been leaning against a pillar staring dreamily at the dancing couples, when she spotted him near one of the doors at the rear of the gymnasium.

Her heart had done a double somersault inside her breast, and her breath had frozen in her throat as she gazed at his handsome figure silhouetted against the midnight blue sky. A cavalcade of emotions had washed over her as she watched him slowly scan the room.

He was looking for her. She could feel it in her bones and as she waited for him to locate her, a shiver of anticipation and longing had raced up her spine.

'No!' The sharp denial was little more than a hoarse whisper, but it was enough to jolt Shay out of her reverie and off the painful path her memories were taking her. With a muttered oath, she moved away from the window and after undressing, climbed into bed.

Sleep, however, was the furthest thing from her mind. She tossed and turned, struggling to keep the memories at bay, finding it an almost impossible task.

Calmly, she tried to tell herself that there was little likelihood of Reeve's ever finding out that Mandy was his daughter. And even if she told him the truth, she doubted he'd believe her. Not when on the night he'd made love to her, she'd assured him she was protected, that she'd been taking birth control pills prescribed for her by a gynecologist.

4

Shay added the egg and buttermilk mixture to the bowl of dry ingredients, and with a wooden spoon, began to stir the batter. Pancakes and bacon were a Sunday-morning ritual for her and Mandy, and with the bacon already cooked and keeping warm in the oven, Shay went to work on the pancakes, having adjusted her usual recipe to accommodate her two guests.

As her thoughts turned to Reeve and Emma, her confident strokes slowed, and not for the first time she wondered just how she would get through the next three weeks.

'Good morning. Mmm, something smells good.'

Shay's fingers fumbled the wooden spoon in her hand, and silently she said a prayer of thanks for the simple fact that she had her back to Reeve, preventing him from seeing her reaction.

Steadying herself, she turned to greet him. 'Good morning,' she replied, sounding much calmer than she felt. 'There's bacon in the oven, and the pancakes will be ready in a few minutes.'

'Sounds wonderful. I'm starving,' Reeve replied.

Dressed in a pair of beige cotton slacks and a green and white short-sleeved shirt, his hair still damp from the shower, he looked stunningly handsome. Beside him, clutching her rag doll, stood Emma, wearing red shorts and a red and white T-shirt. In her hair was a small red barrette.

''Morning, Emma,' Shay added, giving the child a friendly smile, but Emma didn't meet her gaze. 'I hope you found your rooms to your liking and that you slept well,' she said, shifting her attention to Reeve.

'I'm not sure whether it was the sea air or just jet lag, but I slept like a log,'

Reeve said. 'And I didn't hear a peep from Emma.' He flashed a smile at his daughter.

'That's good,' Shay responded as she turned back to the stove and began to spoon batter onto the hot skillet. 'These will only take a few minutes, then I'll set a table in the dining room.'

'There's no need for that, surely,' Reeve quickly asserted, surprised and strangely hurt that Shay had even considered the option.

'Well, no . . . I suppose not,' Shay replied, feeling her face grow warm with embarrassment. 'I just thought — ' She broke off, not wanting to add that her purpose had been to try to maintain a formal distance between them. She hadn't been sure just how to behave toward Reeve. After all, he was a paying customer.

The back door opened and Mandy joined them. 'Here's the newspaper, Mom,' she said, dropping it onto the kitchen counter. 'Hi, Emma.' Mandy smiled as she greeted her half sister.

'Want to come and see Patches? She's sleeping on my bed.'

Emma glanced up at her father, obviously looking for his approval.

Reeve nodded. 'Why don't you leave Susie here with me?' he suggested casually. Since awakening, Emma had once again reverted to holding on to the rag doll, and while he'd made no comment, Reeve was anxious to see if Emma could be persuaded to part with the doll.

Emma hesitated, but only for a moment. Thrusting the rag doll at her father, she turned and followed Mandy from the kitchen.

'That's a relief,' Reeve commented.

'I'm sorry . . . ?' Shay said.

'When Emma woke this morning, the first thing she reached for was Susie,' Reeve explained. 'I thought we were back to square one, but she relinquished it willingly enough just now.' He set Emma's rag doll on one of the kitchen chairs. 'The girls certainly seem to have hit it off,' he commented.

'Mmm,' Shay said noncommittally as she watched the bubbles forming on the pancakes.

'Is there anything I can do?' Reeve asked, his voice coming from directly behind her now.

Shay felt her pulse jitter in response to his nearness. 'Ah . . . no . . . thanks,' she answered, concentrating on flipping the pancakes. 'There's coffee on the counter, or if you prefer, there's a pitcher of fresh orange juice on the table. Sit down and help yourself,' she invited and swallowed her sigh of relief as he retreated to the table.

Pulling out a chair, Reeve sat down and poured a glass of juice. Taking a sip, he let his gaze glide over Shay. On her feet she wore a pair of thonged leather sandals and her long lightly tanned legs disappeared into a pair of white walking shorts, which accentuated the firmness of her buttocks as well as the narrowness of her waist. A sleeveless tank top in contrasting shades of blue and green was tucked into the top of her shorts and Reeve found his gaze lingering on the gentle swell of her breast.

Reeve smiled as he noted the way she'd tucked her hair behind her ears, a sure sign of concentration that allowed him an unobstructed view of the classic outline of her cheekbones and the fragile curve of her neck.

As he studied her, Reeve found himself wondering at the tension he could see in the set of her shoulders, and the pulse throbbing just below her left ear. His own pulse, he was surprised to discover, had picked up speed. Not for the first time, he silently acknowledged that Shay had blossomed and matured into a stunningly attractive woman.

'Is breakfast ready yet, Mom?' Mandy's question cut through Reeve's musings.

'These pancakes are ready, and there are more on the way,' Shay announced, turning and setting the plate of hotcakes on the kitchen table. 'I'll get the bacon.'

'Didn't I see a bowl of strawberries in the fridge?' Mandy asked.

'You did,' Shay replied. 'Would you get them for me, please?' she asked. She slid her hands into oven gloves and retrieved the plate of bacon.

'This brings back memories,' Reeve said as he helped Emma into the chair beside him.

'Memories?' Shay repeated, casting a questioning glance over her shoulder.

'Of Sunday-morning breakfasts at our house when I was a child,' Reeve replied. 'My mother cooked a breakfast just like this, and we'd sit around the kitchen table, sometimes for the best part of the morning, eating and talking.' Reeve came to a halt, a smile of reminiscence on his handsome features.

'Sunday mornings were never that relaxed around here,' Shay said after she'd flipped the second batch of pancakes. 'Aunt Izzy would be busy cooking for all the guests, and I'd be rushing back and forth from the tables in the dining room, trying to remember who'd ordered what. I wasn't the best of waitresses.'

'Will I have to be a waitress, too?' Mandy asked, taking her seat at the table.

Shay smiled at her daughter and shook her head. 'No, at least not till you're a bit older,' she said, sliding the last of the pancakes onto a second plate and turning off the burner.

'When are you planning to open for business?' Reeve asked as he forked several pancakes from the platter and dropped them onto Emma's plate.

'Next weekend,' Shay replied. 'It's the August holiday weekend,' she went on. She'd actually hoped to have the Vacancy sign up this weekend, but when Alice asked if she'd cater her wedding reception, Shay had been more than happy to oblige. The extra money she'd earned had been spent on advertising the upcoming opening of the bed-and-breakfast inn in several of the larger newspapers both on the island and on the mainland.

'Mom, can Emma and I go down to the beach and play after breakfast?' Mandy asked.

'I don't think so, darling,' Shay responded. 'I have some work to do here, and Emma's father may have other plans,' she added, hoping this was indeed true, not at all looking forward to having Reeve underfoot.

'I'm sure Emma would love to go to the beach and play, Mandy,' Reeve said. 'But your mother's right, I have a few things to take care of in town this morning, and I thought I'd show Emma around the clinic where I'll be working.'

'You're going to be working in Stuart's Cove?' Mandy asked, looking surprised.

'Yes,' Reeve said. 'I'm taking over for Dr. Walker while he and Alice are on their honeymoon,' he explained.

Mandy turned to her mother. 'I thought you said there was a lady doctor coming from Vancouver.'

'There was,' Shay replied, 'but she

had an accident and won't be able to make it.'

Mandy glanced at Emma and a smile broke over her features. 'Does that mean you and Emma are going to be staying here with us until Alice and Dr. Walker get back?' she asked, excitement in her voice now.

'Yes, it does,' Reeve replied.

'Cool!' Mandy exclaimed, grinning widely at Emma.

'I'm glad you approve,' Reeve said, a hint of humor in his voice. He glanced at Shay in time to see the flicker of apprehension that flashed in her eyes. 'Maybe we can take that walk to the beach when we get back,' he suggested.

'Okay,' Mandy replied. 'And I can show Emma my tree house, too.'

'Tree house,' Reeve repeated, his gaze sliding to meet Shay's. 'Is that the same one I helped you build?'

'You helped my mom build the tree house?' Mandy quickly cut in before Shay could answer.

'I certainly did,' Reeve said with a

smile. 'Not that your mother wanted my help, mind you.' He chuckled softly at the memory.

'That's because I was quite capable of building the tree house on my own,' Shay felt inclined to point out. Aunt Izzy had been the one who'd balked at a twelve-year-old girl using a saw, and a hammer and nails, without proper adult supervision, and had asked Reeve if he would mind helping Shay with the construction.

'You'd never have managed to carry the plywood up there by yourself,' Reeve remarked, enjoying the chance to tease Shay.

'Hah!' Shay countered, rising to the bait. 'If you recall, I'd hauled most of it up before you even came on the scene. I knew how to use a hammer just as well as you did,' she scoffed. 'I didn't need your help,' she added, fired up by the old argument that had been the bone of contention between them the summer she was twelve.

'I know how to use a hammer, too,'

100

Mandy proudly asserted, jumping into the fray. 'Mom showed me.' She grinned at Shay. 'But she won't let me use it to put a roof on the tree house,' Mandy concluded with a sigh.

Reeve's low rumble of laughter had Shay silently fuming. Ever since Mandy had discovered the tree house, she'd been pestering Shay to put a roof on it, in the faint hope of being granted permission to spend the night in the branches of the sprawling old oak.

Shay met Reeve's gaze across the table, noting the twinkle of merriment dancing in the depths of his gray eyes. As their gazes locked, she felt her mouth go dry and her breath catch in her throat at the sizzling tension suddenly vibrating between them.

Awareness skimmed across Reeve's nerve endings, catching him by surprise. He could see by the way Shay's eyes darkened to a midnight blue that she was equally aware of the sexual tension simmering in the air.

'If your mother doesn't have time,

maybe Emma and I can help you put a roof on the tree house,' Reeve offered, having managed to drag his eyes away from Shay and onto Mandy.

'Would you?' Mandy's eyes were wide with excitement at the prospect, reminding Reeve for a moment of how Emma had looked before the accident whenever he'd promised her a special treat.

'I'd love to,' he replied sincerely. 'As long as it's all right with your mother, of course.'

'Mom! Please, please say it's all right,' Mandy begged. 'Then maybe one night while Emma's here, we can . . .' Mandy ground to a halt, possibly feeling that she might be pushing her luck.

Shay met her daughter's eyes and bit back a sigh of exasperation. 'If Dr. Walker has time to help put a roof on the tree house, then I certainly won't object,' Shay said with as much grace as she could muster.

'Dr. Walker?' Mandy's expression was

one of confusion.

'My name's Dr. Walker, too, like my father's, but you can call me Reeve,' he invited, flashing Mandy a smile.

★   ★   ★

When Reeve and Emma departed a short time later, Shay began to clear away the breakfast dishes and load the dishwasher. Outside, the sun was slowly making its ascent into the sky, pushing the temperature into the eighties.

'Emma's dad is really nice, isn't he, Mom?' Mandy commented as she fed the kitten.

'Yes, he is,' Shay replied, keeping her tone even, hearing the hint of longing in her daughter's voice.

'I wonder why Emma's mom didn't come with them,' Mandy said after a moment's silence.

Shay closed the dishwasher and crossed to where Mandy stood stroking Patches. Crouching, she faced her daughter. 'Emma's mother died in a car accident a few months ago,' Shay explained, believing it would be better for Mandy to know the truth for fear she might ask Reeve the same question, or chatter to Emma about her mother.

'Oh, poor Emma,' Mandy said. 'No wonder she looks so sad and doesn't want to talk. She probably misses her mom a whole lot.'

'I'm sure she does,' Shay replied, touched by Mandy's obvious compassion. 'Listen, sweetie, I have work to do. If you want to give me a hand, fine, if not, you know the rules . . . '

'I know. Don't go to the beach by myself. Stay in the yard and check in with you now and then,' Mandy reeled off.

Shay nodded. 'Oh, and don't forget, if you do go out . . . '

'Wear my baseball hat and put on sunscreen,' Mandy said with an exaggerated sigh.

'Good girl,' Shay responded before dropping a kiss on her daughter's head. 'I'll be upstairs. Yell if you need me.'

Up on the second floor, Shay drew level with the door to Reeve's room. She hesitated for a moment before moving to the room she'd allocated to Emma. Once inside, Shay crossed to the single bed and began to smooth the sheets and tug the lightweight cotton comforter into place.

Picking up the two white socks peeking out from under the bed, Shay tucked them into the shoes sitting next to the bedside table. After a brief glance around to make sure everything was tidy, she walked through the connecting door into Reeve's room.

The moment she entered, she was instantly aware of the musky masculine scent that belonged to Reeve lingering in the air, a scent that had her muscles tensing and her pulse racing. As her gaze fell on the double bed with its white sheets in disarray, an image of Reeve's naked body entwined with hers suddenly flashed into her head.

'No!' The word burst forth of its own volition and it was all she could do not to turn and run. Drawing a deep steadying breath, she wiped the erotic images from her mind, resolutely reminding herself that ten years ago after making love to her on the beach, Reeve hadn't kept his promise to call her. He'd flown off to New York without even bothering to say goodbye.

With hands that were trembling, Shay applied herself to the task of making the bed Reeve had slept in. Once the task was completed, she checked to make sure everything was in order before retreating, with some relief, to the bathroom across the hall.

Her feeling of relief, however, was short-lived as she was again bombarded with the alluring masculine scent that was Reeve's alone. Muttering under her breath, Shay quickly cleaned and tidied the bathroom and after hanging up fresh towels from the linen closet, she hurried downstairs.

★ ★ ★

By three o'clock in the afternoon, Shay was sitting on a beach blanket hugging her knees, watching Mandy in her bathing suit playing in the small tidal pools near the water's edge.

Her glance drifted out across the water where she could see several sailboats bobbing on the waves. As the faint off-shore breeze tugged playfully at her hair, Shay felt a sense of peace, a sense of having come home.

The small secluded cove was bordered on one side by two huge boulders known locally as the Twin Rocks, and on the other side by a rugged headland jutting out to sea. This stretch of beach was generally much quieter than the larger beach next to the marina and more accessible to tourists staying in Stuart's Cove.

Closing her eyes, Shay inhaled deeply, drawing in the tangy sea air before releasing it in a sigh that was overflowing with contentment.

'Mind if we join you?'

Reeve's deep familiar voice brought

Shay's eyes open in a flash, and the feelings of peace and contentment she'd been enjoying instantly evaporated, replaced by an awareness that sent a tremor racing through her.

'Emma, Mandy's right there by the tidal pools.' Reeve crouched beside his daughter to point to where Mandy was playing near the shoreline. 'Want me to walk with you?' he asked. Emma shook her head and scampered off. 'I didn't disturb you, did I?' Reeve went on as he dropped onto the blanket beside Shay.

'No,' Shay lied as she tried with every appearance of casualness to retreat to the edge of the blanket. Reeve had changed into a pair of gray shorts and Shay felt her pulse trip over itself at the sight of his long muscular legs stretched out beside her.

'Thanks for leaving the door unlocked,' Reeve said lowering himself onto an elbow, and angling his body toward her. 'Though I'm not sure that's altogether a safe practice these days.'

'I forgot to give you a key,' Shay

responded in defense of her action. 'And besides, the crime rate isn't very high around here,' she told him. 'How was everything at the clinic?' She changed the topic, keeping her gaze on the two children who were busy making little running forays in and out of the water.

'Terrific,' Reeve replied. 'I'm impressed at the smooth and efficient way the clinic runs. My father certainly found a great office administrator in Brenda,' he commented. 'She came by to see Dr. Billings but got me instead. Now I'm the owner of this electronic pager.' He patted the small black device clipped to his belt.

'Does that mean you're on call around the clock?' Shay asked.

'According to Brenda, all medical-emergency calls are received at the switchboard at the hospital in Fern-haven, fifty miles away. Depending on the location of the emergency, the call is then routed through the clinic to me, or to the hospital's own emergency units,' he explained.

'I see,' Shay said, equally impressed by the system he'd just described.

'Of course, being the summer season, and with all the vacationers in the area, the number of emergencies does tend to rise,' Reeve said. 'But I don't anticipate any major problems.' He watched Mandy and Emma come running up the beach toward them. 'Hello, girls. What's up?' he asked, easing himself into a sitting position.

'Emma and me are going to look for shells,' Mandy said. 'Is it all right if we walk to the Twin Rocks and back?' she asked, turning to Shay.

At the mention of the Twin Rocks, Shay's glance flew to meet Reeve's and she felt her stomach muscles tighten.

Ten years ago, on a warm summer's night in June, Reeve had made love to her in the small alcove where the two rocks appeared to overlap. But as she gazed into the depths of his steel gray eyes in search of a reaction, she saw nothing that might indicate he even remembered their passionate encounter.

A pain intense and unwanted suddenly clutched at Shay's heart, but she forced herself to ignore it. She turned to Mandy who stood with Emma waiting for a reply. 'That's rather a long way, don't you think?' Shay managed to keep her tone even. 'Why don't the two of you build a sand castle right here, instead?' she suggested, silently wishing she could gather up her things and retreat to the house where she could nurse her wounds in private.

Mandy scrunched up her face in response to her mother's suggestion. 'It's not that far,' she replied. 'And we promise to turn around and come right back, don't we, Emma?'

Emma nodded solemnly, her blue eyes, so like Mandy's, silently pleading with Shay to give her assent.

'I don't — ' Shay began.

'Why don't we all go?' Reeve cut in, effectively bringing Shay's glance back to those cool gray eyes. Suddenly, the air seemed to be humming with tension and it was all Shay could do not to drop her gaze.

'Can we, Mom? Please?' Mandy begged, diverting Shay's attention away from Reeve.

'That's a great idea,' Shay announced with forced brightness, anxious to give Reeve the impression that nothing was amiss. 'A walk will give us an appetite for dinner,' she added, all the while thinking that she'd rather walk over a bed of hot coals than return with Reeve to the Twin Rocks.

'Can me and Emma run on ahead?' Mandy asked.

'Sure, off you go,' Reeve replied, rising to his feet in one athletic movement. 'Your mother and I will be right behind you.'

Mandy grabbed Emma's hand, and the two of them headed down the sand.

'Give me your hand,' Reeve said, turning to Shay.

'I can manage, thanks,' Shay responded politely. Careful to avoid any contact with him, she hopped to her feet. As she did, one of her leather sandals slipped from her foot, throwing her momentarily off-balance, and all at once she found herself stumbling against Reeve's tall muscular frame.

At the unexpected contact, Shay's heart leaped into her throat, and when his hands clasped her shoulders to steady her, a tingling heat began to spiral through her, awakening every cell in its path.

'Careful,' Reeve admonished gently, his head only inches from her own, his breath fanning her ear, his erotic male scent sending her senses spinning out of control.

'Thank you. I'm fine,' she lied, fighting to clamp down on the urge to wrench free of his grasp. His nearness and the touch of his hands were evoking a response she'd never thought to feel again.

Ever since her encounter with Reeve ten years ago, she had studiously avoided close relationships with men, content simply to enjoy them as friends, keeping them at arm's length, never allowing anyone close enough physically or emotionally for fear of having her heart broken a second time.

'Are you sure?' Reeve asked, reluctant to let her go. He could see panic flickering in the depths of her pale blue eyes and was puzzled by it.

'Of course I'm sure,' Shay replied, an edge to her tone now, almost sagging with relief when he released her. 'We'd better catch up with the girls.' She moved away, annoyed at the husky note she could hear in her voice.

Her legs felt like wet strands of seaweed and with every step she took threatened to give way under her. Her heart, too, continued to thunder against her rib cage as if she'd completed a marathon.

Reeve caught up with her in three easy strides. 'Here, put this on.' He held out the wide-brimmed straw hat she'd brought with her to the beach.

Shay accepted the hat without a

word, glad of its protection from the hot sun, and glad that she could angle it a little and block her view of Reeve's tall imposing figure walking beside her.

'So, tell me. How are you enjoying being back in Stuart's Cove?' Reeve asked a few moments later.

'I love it,' Shay replied without hesitation. She hadn't realized just how much she'd missed the rugged beauty of the area, or the sights and sounds of the ocean crashing practically on her doorstep.

'You don't miss France?' he queried. 'I've heard the countryside is very beautiful.'

'It is.' She confirmed. 'But it's the people I miss the most,' she continued, her thoughts drifting now to Aunt Izzy's friends — those who'd rallied around them when they'd first arrived in France and the friends she'd made while working at the restaurant in Provence.

'You said yesterday that you weren't married,' Reeve went on, more than a little curious to know something about Mandy's father. 'Does that mean you and Mandy's father are divorced?'

Though Shay knew she shouldn't be surprised by his directness, she hadn't expected to be faced with the prospect of having to lie to him, at least not so soon.

Her gaze lit on the girls, less than twenty yards away, crouching to inspect something lying on the sand. 'What did you find?' Shay called, breaking into a run, knowing she was simply postponing the inevitable but glad of an excuse not to answer Reeve's question.

'It's a crab,' Mandy replied, flashing her mother a smile. 'He's trying to protect himself. See?' She pointed to where the crab, pincers poised to strike, stood his ground.

'Let's leave him be,' Shay suggested as she sidestepped the small crustacean.

'He looks more angry than frightened,' Reeve commented, crouching beside the girls to take a closer look at the midsize Dungeness crab bravely defending himself against an onslaught of humans.

'How do you know it's a he?' Mandy asked.

Reeve grinned. 'I don't. Let's find out.' With a movement as swift as any magician's, his hand swooped down to capture the crab, holding it at arm's length, careful to avoid the creature's flailing pincers.

'Wow, that was fast!' Mandy gazed in open admiration at the man who was her father. Watching the brief interplay, Shay felt a momentary stab of both guilt and regret, but resolutely shoved them aside, reminding herself that in a few short weeks, Reeve and Emma would be winging their way back to New York and out of their lives.

Carefully turning the crab over, Reeve revealed its underside. 'Do you see the wide V shape?' he asked, glancing first at Emma then at Mandy.

Both girls nodded.

'That tells me it's a female,' Reeve said to his enthralled audience. 'If it was a boy crab, the V shape would be noticeably narrower,' he explained. 'I think it's time we let Miss Crab get on with what she was doing.' He set the struggling crab back onto the sand and released it.

The girls watched as the indignant crab sidestepped her way toward the water. 'Come on, Emma,' Mandy said, tugging at her half sister's hand. 'There's bound to be some shells nearer to the rocks,' she said, and once again the girls scampered ahead.

Reeve rose from his crouched position and fell into step with Shay. 'You didn't answer my question,' he said a moment later, shattering any hope she'd had that he wouldn't pursue the subject.

'That's because I don't think it's any of your business,' Shay replied, silently rationalizing that if she refused to answer his questions, she wouldn't be forced into telling him a lie.

Reeve threw a sideways glance at Shay, surprised not only by her brittle tone, but by her refusal to answer what to him seemed a reasonable enough question. 'Does Mandy ever see her father?' he asked, deciding to change tactics, but growing more curious now about the child's father.

Shay came to a halt and turned to face him. 'Why do you care?' she asked, wishing now she hadn't agreed to accompany him on the walk, that she'd stayed behind and thus avoided this conversation altogether.

★   ★   ★

Reeve frowned, puzzled at the defensive note in her voice. 'I care because I like Mandy, she's a sweet kid,' he replied sincerely. 'Look at the way she's accepted Emma's silence without making Emma feel in any way unusual or awkward. I wish some of the doctors she's seen in the past three months treated her half as well,' Reeve said. 'Any man would be proud to have Mandy as his daughter, me included.'

Shay stared at Reeve in stunned silence. *She is your daughter!* The words screamed inside her head, but she bit down on the inner softness of her mouth, fighting to prevent herself from blurting out the truth.

'Listen, Shay — ' Reeve's tone softened when he saw the strange look on her face ' — I didn't mean to upset you. You obviously don't want to talk about Mandy's father, and I respect that. All I can say is he must have hurt you deeply.' He stopped, wanting more than ever now to know the man responsible for causing the pain he could see clouding the depths of her blue eyes.

The urge to haul her into his arms and comfort her was strong, but he resisted it. 'There was a time when you came to me with all your troubles.' He kept his tone light, remembering those times with warmth and affection. 'My shoulder's still there, if you ever need it. Isn't that what friends are for?'

The hard lump of emotion clogging

Shay's throat made it impossible for her to speak. Blinking away the tears stinging her eyes, she shook her head, telling herself over and over she was doing the right thing, that telling Reeve about Mandy would only create more problems, resolutely refusing to listen to the little voice inside her head saying she was wrong.

5

'The girls must have found something,' Reeve said. 'Mandy is calling.' Turning, he acknowledged his daughter's shouts with a wave of his hand. 'I'll check it out,' he added before striding off, giving Shay some much-needed space and time to regain her composure.

A stray tear traced a path down her cheek and Shay brushed it away before taking several deep steadying breaths. Crouching on the sand, she removed her thongs, all the while berating herself for not handling Reeve's questions with more poise and sophistication.

She should have lied. She should have fabricated a story and satisfied his curiosity, preventing any further discussion of the topic. By failing to supply him with an adequate answer, she'd accomplished what she'd most wanted to avoid. She'd piqued his interest and she knew, without a doubt, that the subject of Mandy's father would return to haunt her.

Reeve's comment about coming to him with her troubles had brought an ache to her heart and a longing for those days of her childhood when her problems, though no less important to her then, had been far less complex.

Back then, he'd been the big brother she'd never had, always willing to listen, never judging or criticizing. The only subject she hadn't been able to talk to him about had been her growing feelings for him, feelings that were in no way sisterly, feelings that kept her awake at night dreaming of what it would be like to feel his lips on hers.

And now with her aunt gone, there was no one she could talk to, no one she could go to and ask for advice, and Shay felt more than a little lost and lonely.

With a sigh, she stood up, and with her thongs in her hand, began to make her way toward the threesome kneeling on the sand near the edge of the first of the Twin Rocks where it emerged from the wet ground.

'Mom! Look at the shells I found.' Mandy hopped to her feet and came to meet her. 'Aren't they pretty?' Her daughter held out her hand for Shay's inspection.

'They're lovely, darling,' Shay enthused as she gazed down at a handful of clam-shells and one large oyster shell partially covered with tiny barnacles. 'Did you find some, too, Emma?' Shay asked, noticing Emma hovering nearby.

'Show Mandy's mom what you found, sweetheart.' Reeve flashed Shay a grateful smile as he gently nudged Emma toward her.

'Emma found a shell that looks like a tiny hat,' Mandy said as Emma took several steps in their direction, tenta-tively opening her hand to show Shay.

'You're right. It does look like a little hat.' Shay smiled at the child. 'Oh . . . and there's an agate.' Shay pointed to the small opaque stone nestled in

Emma's hand. 'Those are very hard to find. You did well to spot it,' she praised. Emma's eyes glowed with pleasure and the beginnings of a smile began to tug at the corners of her mouth.

'Want me to put your treasures in my pocket, Emma?' Reeve asked, and at the question Emma turned to her father, her face expressionless once more. 'You don't want to lose them, do you?'

Emma shook her head.

'Would you look after mine, too?' Mandy asked, gazing up at Reeve, a hopeful look on her upturned face.

'I'd be happy to,' Reeve replied, his face creasing into a warm smile.

That Mandy had taken a shine to Reeve was both obvious and understandable. Up until now, there had been no father figure in her young life, no positive male influence, no man to look up to. From what Shay had seen of Reeve, he appeared to be a loving and doting father and she couldn't really blame Mandy for wanting a share of his attention.

'Let's see what we can find at the water's edge.' Reeve turned toward the water, with the girls following close behind.

Shay climbed the gentle slope of the smooth gray rock in search of a flat place to sit down. From her vantage point, she watched Reeve and his daughters scan the wet sand for more treasures as the waves lapped gently at their feet.

Suddenly, Reeve came to a halt and crouched. He began to brush away sand to reveal something which had been half-buried. The girls quickly joined him and, heads together, they inspected his find before he placed it back on the sand.

Rising to his full height once more, Reeve reached for Emma's hand and lifted her up and over a larger wave as it broke around them. Shay heard Mandy's squeal of surprise as the water splashed her daughter's legs.

Still holding Emma's hand, Reeve

turned to Mandy and offered her his free hand. Shay felt as if her heart was being squeezed in a vise when, after the briefest of hesitations, Mandy accepted her father's hand.

Shay watched Reeve walk hand in hand with his daughters along the water's edge. Even from a distance, she could see Mandy's animated expression as she chattered nonstop to her father, and all at once, Shay was bombarded with memories of times spent with her own father whom she'd adored.

Her parents had been killed in a car accident when she was ten and although eighteen years had passed since their deaths, she still remembered how special they'd made her feel, especially her father.

Some of her best-loved memories were of the countless hours she'd spent with him in his workshop. A carpenter by trade, Patrick O'Brien had been the one who'd taught Shay how to use some of his tools. He'd been a patient teacher and a loving father, always praising her efforts, giving assistance whenever she became frustrated, quietly keeping his fatherly eye on her, helping in no small way to build both her self-confidence and her self-esteem.

She still missed him and her mother, too, remembering the warm, tender and loving relationship her parents had shared. Patrick O'Brien had adored his wife. They'd been so happy together, so much in love that there had been times when Shay had felt a little left out.

Young as she'd been, she'd instinctively sensed that the love her parents shared had been something rare and precious and, as she grew older, she'd dreamed of one day knowing a love like theirs.

But she'd discovered the hard way that dreams rarely come true, that happily-ever-after endings only belonged in the pages of the romance novels she loved to read.

'Mom!' Mandy's voice cut through her wayward thoughts and she blinked away the remaining moisture from her eyes as her daughter attempted to scramble up the slippery rock face toward her.

'Stay there, I'm coming down,' Shay said and quickly slid down the rock to land beside her daughter. 'Did you find any more treasures?'

'Reeve found a sand dollar,' her daughter reported. 'He showed Emma and me all the pretty markings, but we had to put it back in the water 'cause he said if we took it home, it would die, that it's a living thing.'

'He's right,' Shay said.

'I think we should head back,' Reeve said as he and Emma joined them. 'I have a few phone calls to make.'

Shay nodded and once again they fell into step together. To Shay's relief, the girls kept pace with them throughout the journey back. From time to time, Shay darted a glance at Reeve from beneath the rim of her straw hat, but he appeared to be deep in thought.

Back at the inn, they each rinsed away the sand from their feet before venturing inside. Reeve and Emma disappeared upstairs and Shay ushered Mandy off to her room to change out of her wet bathing suit.

Alone in the kitchen, Shay began to prepare a green salad to accompany the salmon steaks she'd removed from the freezer earlier.

'Mom, Emma and me are going to play outside on the swings,' Mandy said.

Shay glanced over her shoulder in time to see Mandy and Emma cross to the door. 'Okay,' she responded. 'Ah . . . where's Emma's father?'

'He's upstairs in his room talking on the telephone,' Mandy replied. 'I told him where we were going,' she added before her mother could ask.

'Fine. I'll call you when supper's ready,' Shay said before turning back to her task of washing the vegetables.

Shay was adding fresh lemon juice to the mixture of olive oil and freshly chopped herbs when Reeve joined her.

'And what culinary delight is in store

for us tonight?' he asked in a teasing tone as he came up behind her.

She tried unsuccessfully to ignore the ripple of awareness that jolted through her in reaction to the sound of his voice and his proximity. Willing her heart to slow down, she managed a fleeting smile. 'Grilled salmon and a mixed green salad,' Shay said. 'This is just a quick and easy salad dressing. I'm not one for using store-bought dressings.' She crossed to the stove to turn the oven on to broil.

'Is there anything I can do? Shall I set the table?' Reeve asked.

'Yes, thank you,' Shay replied, warmed by his offer. 'There's cutlery in the top drawer and place mats are in the next one down,' she said, pointing to the row of drawers on the opposite counter.

Crossing to the fridge, Shay removed the dish containing the salmon steaks, which had been marinating in a spicy lemon-juice brine since early that afternoon. With a pair of tongs, Shay carefully placed the steaks onto a grill and in a matter of moments slid them into the oven under the broiler.

'Shay, there's something I want to ask you,' Reeve said. At the serious tone in his voice, Shay felt her heart skip a beat. She carefully schooled her features, preparing herself for the lie she must speak. Turning from the stove, she met his gaze, but his expression was unreadable.

'What is it?' she asked cautiously, pleased that her voice didn't betray any of the anxiety flitting through her.

'Would you mind very much looking after Emma for me while I'm at the clinic? I know it's asking a lot,' he hurried on. 'But I don't think she's ready yet for a day-care situation, and she and Mandy seem to have hit it off . . . '

Relief washed over her and she smiled. 'Of course I don't mind,' she said. 'Mandy's always complaining that there are no other children in the area for her to play with.'

Reeve took several steps toward her. 'Thanks, Shay. This really means a lot to me,' he said. 'I'll pay the current rates, of course. And no arguments, please,' he added before Shay could even think about responding.

'No arguments,' she replied, beginning to think that Reeve and Emma's arrival in Stuart's Cove was steadily turning into a blessing in disguise, financially at least.

★ ★ ★

For the week that followed, the days fell into something of a pattern. Each morning, Mandy and Emma, both early risers, would share breakfast with their father before he left for the clinic.

Throughout the morning, the children would play in the yard or in the tree house while Shay cleaned and tidied and prepared the remainder of the rooms in readiness for the upcoming opening of O'Brien's Bed and Breakfast Inn.

Hot, sunny skies prevailed for the entire week, and each afternoon, when the heat of the day was a little less intense, Shay would walk to the beach with the girls and watch while they built sand castles, or ran in and out of the tidal pools or lazed around on the sand. When she became too hot, she would run into the ocean to cool off, and the girls would join her, staying close to shore, content to jump through the smaller waves breaking onto the sand.

When Reeve returned from the clinic in the late afternoon, he would take a quick, refreshing shower then sit with the girls, listening while Mandy recounted in elaborate detail how they'd spent their day.

Leaving the children to watch their favorite television program, he'd join Shay in the kitchen. Her initial reaction had been to reject his offer of help, due for the most part to the fact that she found his presence infinitely disturbing and coupled with the fear that he might once again broach the subject of

Mandy's father and start asking questions, questions she wasn't prepared to answer.

But Shay discovered that Reeve wasn't a man who took no for an answer, and it wasn't long before she had to admit that she looked forward to the time they spent together in the kitchen.

That he enjoyed cooking was obvious and Shay was surprised and impressed at how knowledgeable he was about herbs and spices. As they worked together, the friendship that had been such an important part of her life when she'd first moved to Stuart's Cove at the age of ten slowly reestablished itself, and silently Shay told herself that Reeve's friendship was all she wanted, all she needed.

But as the weekend approached, Shay found it increasingly difficult to ignore the old longings stirring to life inside her. And it didn't help that with each day that passed, she watched her daughter fall deeper under her father's spell.

After supper each evening, Reeve would take the children for a walk along the beach. Shay politely declined his nightly invitations to join them, trying with some modicum of success to maintain a distance between them.

But watching Reeve with his daughters, seeing the warmth, the love, the tenderness he bestowed on them, she knew the wall she'd built around her heart was beginning to crumble.

And when she glimpsed a look of anxiety in the depths of his eyes, an anxiety brought on by Emma's continued silence, an anxiety he was studiously careful never to let his daughter see, Shay found it almost impossible to squash the impulse to reach out and comfort him.

★ ★ ★

'I heard a car,' Mandy said for what must have been the twentieth time in the past hour.

Shay listened for a moment. 'No, I

don't think so,' she responded with a sigh, looking up from the recipe book she'd been browsing through.

It was well past noon on Saturday, and before leaving for the clinic that morning, Reeve had helped Shay hang the new bed-and-breakfast sign and the Vacancy sign on the post at the front of the house.

Using the same colors her aunt had favored on the old signs, Shay had painted the new ones herself. The bright gold lettering of O'Brien's Bed and Breakfast Inn stood out boldly against the pale yellow background and Shay only hoped she would enjoy at least some of the same success her aunt had achieved.

'Why don't you two go and play outside for a while?' Shay suggested.

'Are you sure, Mom?' Mandy hopped down from the kitchen chair where she'd been sitting and came to stand beside Shay.

Shay smiled at her daughter and gently touched her nose. 'I'm sure,' she replied. Mandy had wanted to help her mother greet their first paying guests, but with no customers in sight, the children had become a little restless.

Mandy turned to her sister. 'Come on, Emma,' she said. 'Let's play in the tree house.'

As the back door closed behind the girls, Shay shut the recipe book she'd been perusing and rose from the table. She'd been attempting to plan a menu for the week ahead and with it a list of grocery items she would need, but there seemed little point, especially when there were no customers in sight.

She knew she was foolish to think that the minute the Vacancy sign was up, she would be inundated with tourists looking for a place to stay the night, but that's exactly what she'd been hoping for. As time ticked by, she began to wonder if reopening the bed and breakfast had been such a good idea, after all.

Annoyed at her negative thoughts, Shay resolutely pushed them away. The inn had only been open for business for a little over five hours, and from her own traveling experiences in Europe with her aunt, Shay knew that most travelers generally didn't start looking for accommodation until late in the afternoon.

There was no point moping around. She would make some pies, she decided. Cooking had always been a source of great comfort to her. Opening a cupboard door, she removed a large mixing bowl and in a matter of minutes began to gather together the ingredients she needed for pie crusts.

Forty minutes later, Shay set the four pies — two apple and two raspberry — aside to cool, and drying her hands on a dish towel, she decided to check on the girls.

Closing the kitchen door behind her, she began to cross the courtyard. All at once, a car swung into the yard and Shay felt her heart skip a beat when she saw Reeve seated at the wheel.

'You're finished early today,' she said

when he opened the driver-side door and climbed out.

'The clinic's only open till noon on Saturdays,' Reeve replied. 'I hung around for a while trying to catch up on some paperwork,' he explained, getting out of the car and shrugging out of his jacket. 'Where are the girls?'

'Down at the tree house,' Shay answered. 'I was on my way to check on them.'

'I'll come with you,' Reeve said, tossing his jacket onto the front seat of the car. 'Then I can take a look and see what's needed for a roof,' he went on as he quickly closed the gap between them.

'Don't worry about it,' Shay said, ignoring the quicksilver shiver of alarm that chased along her nerve endings when he drew level with her. 'In fact, I'd be glad if you'd forget all about putting on a roof. Mandy only wants one so she can pressure me into letting her spend the night out there,' she told him as they rounded the corner of the house and headed down the path toward the sprawling old oak sitting at the bottom of the garden.

'I seem to recall that you spent a night out in the tree house yourself,' Reeve said, flashing a teasing smile at her.

'Then you should also remember that I told you it was one of the most unpleasant nights of my life,' Shay countered. 'The wooden floor was so hard I couldn't sleep, and on top of that, the wind rustled through the leaves, making it sound as if someone or something was climbing up the tree.'

'The simple solution would have been to climb down and go back inside to your own room,' Reeve said, a trace of amusement in his voice.

Shay came to a halt and turned to face him. 'I'll have you know, I fought long and hard to get Aunt Izzy to allow me to spend the night there, and I had no intention of letting some spooky little noises made by the wind spoil my victory and send me scurrying back to my bedroom.'

Reeve's low rumble of laughter sent her blood pounding through her veins and a longing tugging at her insides.

'I always wondered why you never noticed that there was no wind that night,' Reeve commented. He grinned at her, watching in fascination as the realization slowly dawned in the depths of her pale blue eyes.

'Are you telling me . . . ? You rat. It was you!' Shay blurted out, her blue eyes shooting daggers at him, her face pink with indignation.

Tempted as he was to laugh, Reeve kept himself in check. 'I thought you knew.' Laughter laced his voice. 'Hey, if it's any consolation, I almost fell and broke my neck. It wasn't easy hugging the trunk with one hand and shaking the branches with the other.'

'It's too bad you didn't fall,' Shay said.

As Reeve gazed at the murderous expression in her eyes, he found himself fighting the urge to cover her mouth with his own and silence her protests.

In an attempt to soothe her ruffled feathers, he brought his hands up to rest on her shoulders, but the moment he touched her, a jolt of awareness, like a current from a live electric wire, ricocheted through him, catching him totally off guard.

Shay's startled gasp told him she felt it, too, and as his eyes locked with hers, the air around them was suddenly crackling with tension.

He was going to kiss her! The realization sent a tremor of need racing through Shay and for the life of her she couldn't move or breathe. She felt his fingers tighten around her upper arm, and as he slowly drew her closer, her heart kicked into high gear, beating a frantic tattoo against her breastbone in heady anticipation of his mouth claiming hers.

Suddenly, the stillness was shattered by the sound of a child's voice.

'Daddy! Daddy! Look at me!'

Reeve froze. He had to be dreaming! Was that Emma's voice he'd heard?

Dropping his hands, he turned toward the direction of the voice and felt his heart leap into his throat at the sight of Emma smiling and waving at him from her vantage point in the opening leading into the tree house.

'Emma! Sweetheart! You spoke!' Reeve said, scarcely able to believe what he'd heard and seen. At his words, a look of surprise mingled with apprehension quickly replaced the happy expression on Emma's face and her smile disappeared.

In five loping strides, Reeve reached the base of the tree and with an agility spurred on by the adrenaline pumping through him, he reached up and scooped his daughter out of the tree house and into his arms, hugging her small frame, trying to contain the feeling of joy sweeping over him.

'Sweetheart. That was terrific!' Reeve spun her around in a dance of pure delight. Although he'd begun to notice a definite change in Emma during the past week, a relaxing of inner tension, and even the hint of a smile on her face, this was the breakthrough he'd been praying for, the breakthrough he'd almost given up hope of ever seeing.

He slowed to a halt. 'Can you say something else for me?' he coaxed, needing to hear her sweet voice again and see her smile.

But as he gazed at his daughter, the relief and happiness sweeping through him evaporated like steam from a kettle when he saw the anxious look on Emma's face.

'What's the matter? Did Daddy frighten you? I'm sorry, sweetie.' Reeve tried to keep his tone even, when all the while he felt like screaming in frustration. 'I'm just so happy that you spoke,' he continued, his voice husky with emotion. 'Can't you say something more for Daddy? Please.'

Emma dropped her chin onto her chest, and Reeve watched in dismay as her lower lip began to quiver and tears pooled in her big blue eyes.

Swallowing the hard lump of emotion clogging his throat, Reeve silently reined in his disappointment. 'Hey, don't cry. It's all right. You don't have to talk if you don't want to. I love you, pumpkin,' he murmured into her baby-soft hair as she buried her face in the curve of his neck.

Shay watched the emotional exchange between Reeve and Emma. She could see the despair and disappointment on his face and wished there was something she could do to alleviate it.

That Emma had spoken was a gigantic step forward for the child, but like the groundhog who poked his head out of his cave only to scurry back inside when he didn't see his shadow, Emma had retreated once more to the safety and security her silent world afforded her.

But Shay felt confident that sometime in the very near future Emma would leave the silent world behind her forever.

'We're proud of you, Emma,' Shay said, wanting to make Emma feel good about the fact that she'd spoken.

'Aren't we, Mandy?'

Mandy, who'd appeared at the top of the ladder, made no response, simply staring at Reeve and Emma, a look of longing on her face, a look that brought a stab of pain to Shay's heart.

'I know!' Shay declared in a loud voice, effectively capturing everyone's attention. 'Why don't we go back to the house and have a glass of that ice-cold lemonade I made this morning?'

'That's a great idea,' Reeve responded. 'What do you say, Emma? Would you like a glass of lemonade?' He gave her an encouraging smile, hoping she would voice her answer.

But Emma only sniffed loudly and after wiping a stray tear from her cheek, nodded in agreement.

'Atta girl!' Reeve said. Hiding his disappointment well, he lowered Emma to the ground.

'Wait for me!' Mandy called.

'I'll lift you down,' Reeve said, and in one quick move he plucked Mandy from the top of the ladder. Mandy's mouth rounded on an O of surprise and pleasure as she grinned delightedly at Reeve as he swung her around before depositing her on the ground next to Emma.

'Race you back to the kitchen,' Mandy challenged, her blue eyes twinkling at him.

'W . . . e . . . ll.' Reeve dragged out the word and stroked his chin thoughtfully as he pretended to consider Mandy's dare. Throwing a quick glance at Emma, he was in time to see a glimmer of excitement in the depths of his daughter's eyes as well as the beginnings of a smile.

Reeve felt his heart contract. It had been a long time since he'd seen a playful look in her eyes, a look of eager anticipation, a look of childish delight, and he realized with a start that ever since the accident, he and everyone around her had been treating her like a porcelain doll, babying her, pampering and protecting her almost to the point of suffocation.

During the past week, however, his responsibilities at the clinic had drawn his focus away from Emma and, with a flash of insight, he sensed that the small but definite changes he'd begun to see in his daughter were a direct result of not being constantly monitored, of being in a much more relaxed environment.

'Do you want to race, too, Emma?' At Reeve's question, Emma's short curls began to dance around her face as she nodded enthusiastically, her earlier anxiety apparently all but forgotten. 'All right. The starting line's right here,' Reeve said, scratching a line across the dirt with the heel of his shoe.

'Mom, you can be the starter,' Mandy suggested, throwing her mother a quick pleading glance.

'That's fine by me,' Shay said and waited a moment for Emma and Mandy to move into line alongside Reeve. 'Get ready! Set! Go!'

Mandy took off like a bullet out of a gun, with Emma a close second. Reeve waited several seconds before making a move, deliberately giving the girls a head start, knowing they'd be too caught up in their own eagerness to win, to notice he was holding back.

Breaking into a run, he jogged after them, shortening his stride, careful not to get too close, while giving the impression that he was indeed running hard. Mandy rounded the corner of the house first, Emma tight on her heels. Reeve brought up the rear.

As they ran across the courtyard, Mandy turned and glanced over her shoulder, an action that broke her rhythm and slowed her footsteps just enough to allow Emma to draw level with her.

Panting a little from the exertion, Reeve watched Mandy grin encouragingly at Emma before holding out her hand. Without any hesitation, Emma grasped Mandy's outstretched hand and together the girls ran the remaining few yards to the door.

'We won! We won!' Mandy yelled as

she and Emma reached the kitchen door at the same time. Emma, breathing hard, was grinning ear to ear, but she didn't join Mandy's vocal celebrations.

'You won, all right.' Reeve slowed to a halt beside them, panting for breath. 'I think you should both sign up for the hundred-yard dash at the next Olympics,' he teased, bending over to rest his hands on his thighs. He'd seen Emma's smile and tempted as he was to reach out and hug her, he held back, content simply to marvel at the miracle and silently celebrate what he hoped was a portent of things to come.

'Mom! Emma and me won,' Mandy boasted when Shay joined them. 'And Reeve thinks we should run in the Olympics,' she told her proudly.

'Way to go, girls!' Shay said. 'As for the Olympics, you'll have to wait a few years before you start training for that. All right! Who wants lemonade?'

'I do! I do!' Mandy was quick to shout.

Emma, still smiling, merely nodded.

The girls followed their father into the kitchen and after gulping down a glass of lemonade each, soon scampered off to play with the kitten in Mandy's bedroom.

Reeve sat staring at the ice cubes melting in the bottom of his glass, trying to convince himself that he had indeed heard his daughter speak and wondering if and when he'd ever hear her again.

'Why so glum?' Shay asked. 'Your daughter spoke. And she hasn't stopped smiling since she came into the kitchen. You should be thrilled.'

Reeve lifted his head and met Shay's gaze. 'So, it wasn't a dream, she did speak,' he responded. 'I wondered if I'd imagined it.'

'No, you definitely didn't imagine it,' Shay confirmed, recalling with vivid clarity the moment when Emma's voice had exploded into the silence, preventing a kiss that would surely have spelled disaster.

'But I don't understand. Why has she withdrawn again?' he asked. 'I thought once she broke the silence . . . ' He sighed heavily.

'The important thing to remember is that Emma did speak,' Shay told him. 'She took a giant leap forward today. She broke the silence. You just have to be patient and not pressure her,' she advised.

'You're right,' Reeve acknowledged. 'I guess I shouldn't have jumped all over her or pushed her to say something else. But I'm afraid I'm a little out of practice at being a full-time parent. I'd forgotten how hard it is.' He ran a hand through his hair, causing a curl to fall across his forehead.

'Forgotten . . . ?' Shay repeated, puzzled by his words and distracted by the urge to comb the wayward curl back into place.

'After our divorce two years ago, Louise retained custody of Emma,' Reeve explained.

Shay felt her heart stumble in

response to his remark. 'You and Louise were divorced?'

'Yes,' Reeve replied. 'And even though I was awarded visiting rights, Louise took great pleasure in depriving me of those, until I rarely saw my own daughter.' Bitterness seeped into his voice now.

'That must have been difficult for you,' Shay said, hearing the pain in every syllable.

'It was unbearable' came the abrupt reply. 'But even worse than that was the way she put Emma in the middle, using her as a bargaining tool. I simply had no choice. I had to back off. And for those two years, I hardly saw Emma at all.' Reeve pushed his chair back and stood up, annoyed with himself for allowing the old memories to affect him. 'The fact that I was Emma's father didn't seem to have any bearing on the matter. And unless I wanted to subject my daughter to more emotional upheaval, there wasn't a damn thing I could do about it.'

Shay turned away from Reeve, moved more than she was willing to admit by the pain and bitterness she could hear in his voice. His anger at having been deprived the right to see Emma touched a raw nerve, and feelings of guilt at the enormity of her own deception suddenly swamped her. For a heart-stopping moment, she was tempted to blurt out the truth.

But all at once, the high-pitched sound of an electronic pager cut through the silence. Reeve instantly snapped to attention, quickly shutting off the device attached to the belt at his waist.

'Must be an emergency,' he said as he reached for the telephone.

Shay watched and waited while Reeve made the call to the clinic switchboard, guessing by the changing expression on his handsome features that something was wrong.

'I've got to go,' Reeve said the minute he'd replaced the receiver. 'I don't know how long I'll be,' he added, flicking a regretful glance in the direction the girls had taken.

'I'll explain to Emma why you had to leave,' Shay said.

Reeve met and held her gaze. 'Thanks,' he said. 'And thanks for listening. One of the drawbacks of being a single parent is not having anyone to talk to.'

'That's true,' she managed to say before he moved to the door.

'I'll see you later,' Reeve said, and with a wave he was gone.

Shay stood for a long moment staring after Reeve. As she'd listened to him talk about how Louise had deprived him of the right to see his daughter, she'd understood what had prompted him to ask her whether Mandy ever saw her father.

But regardless of his reasons, she had to hope that he wouldn't broach the subject of a father's rights again. Because if he did, she wasn't at all sure how much longer she'd be able to hold on to the secret she'd been living with for the past ten years.

6

The sound of a key in the back door woke Shay instantly, causing the book lying open on her lap to slide to the floor with a quiet thud. Glancing at the clock sitting on the bookshelf nearby, she was startled to discover that it was almost midnight.

Bending over, she picked up the fallen book and setting it on the bookshelf, rose and headed to the kitchen.

'Oh! Hello,' Reeve greeted her. 'You're still up. When I saw the light, I thought you'd forgotten to turn it off.'

'I must have dozed off in the chair,' Shay explained, silently telling herself that the quick leap her heart took was simply a result of having her sleep disturbed and had nothing at all to do with Reeve. 'How did it go?' she asked, nothing the tired slump of his shoulders and the weary look in his gray eyes.

'Everything went well,' he told her confidently. 'The patient was a thirteen-year-old kid named Tony. He and his parents are vacationing here in Stuart's Cove. Thankfully, we got him to the hospital before his appendix ruptured.'

'You went with them to Fernhaven?' Shay asked.

'Yes,' Reeve responded. 'I would have been back sooner, but I decided to stay on and see him through the surgery.'

'And is he all right?'

'He's going to be fine,' Reeve replied. 'His mother went in the ambulance with him, and his father was too upset to drive, so I offered him a ride to the hospital in my car,' he explained. 'I just dropped them off at their hotel on my way back.'

'You must be exhausted,' Shay said, warmed by his generosity. 'Can I fix something for you? Did you get a chance to eat?'

'I have eaten, thanks. I grabbed a sandwich in the hospital cafeteria,' Reeve said, then sighed. 'I'm looking forward to having the day off tomorrow. I hadn't realized how hard my father worked. But I must say I'm impressed at how smoothly everything runs,' he added. 'Well, I think I'll say good-night.'

'Wait. Before you go upstairs, I should tell you that Emma's not in her room.'

'She's not? Is she all right?' Reeve turned anxious eyes to meet her gaze.

'She's fine,' Shay assured him. 'When I told her that you'd been called away, she became upset,' she explained, refraining from adding that Emma had burst into tears.

Emma's reaction had startled Shay and instinctively she'd drawn the child into the circle of her arms to comfort her. At first, Emma had stiffened, resisting the embrace, but seconds later she'd held on to Shay as if she might never let go.

'Damn! That's my fault,' Reeve said with a tired sigh. 'I should have talked to her myself before I left.'

'You didn't have much choice,' Shay reminded him, tamping down on the urge to reach out and soothe away the lines of strain she could see etched on his handsome face. 'She settled down. But when it came time for bed, I sensed that she was reluctant to go upstairs by herself, and so I asked if she'd like to spend the night in Mandy's room.'

'She jumped all over that, I bet,' Reeve said, a rueful smile on his face.

Shay nodded, recalling the look of relief and pleasure that had lit up Emma's features at the time.

Reeve ran a hand through his hair. 'Would you mind if I peeked in on her?' he asked, suddenly needing to look at his daughter just to reassure himself that she was indeed all right.

'Of course not,' Shay replied. 'Follow me.' Crossing the kitchen, Shay led the way down the hall leading to Mandy's and her room.

Fearful of waking the girls, Shay dimmed the hall light before nudging open her daughter's bedroom door.

Edging past Shay, Reeve gazed at the children sleeping side by side. Behind him, Shay noticed that both girls had kicked off the lightweight sheet she'd thrown over them earlier and were now lying on their sides in similar sleeping positions, their bodies loosely curled, their hands tucked under their chins.

Shay's heart stumbled to a halt when she saw how alike the children looked as they slept. Other than Mandy's slightly larger body and longer hair, there was little to distinguish between the two of them, and even as Shay rubbed a hand over her heart to make sure it was still beating, she held her breath, waiting for Reeve to turn accusing eyes at her.

But seconds later, when Reeve did turn toward her, the faint smile on his face told her he hadn't noticed the resemblance. Relief made her legs feel weak and she leaned against the door frame for support.

'Sometimes I have a hard time believing she's truly mine,' Reeve said huskily. 'They look so beautiful, so innocent when they're asleep,' he added, his voice little more than a whisper. The low seductive sound sent a tremor racing through Shay. Her pulse reacted, too, gathering speed, making her heart shudder in her breast.

'Yes. They do,' Shay managed to say, though her voice had a breathless quality, a direct result of Reeve's nearness. As she reached forward to grasp the door handle, her body brushed his and at the contact her heart leaped into her throat and a jolt of awareness shot through her, bringing every cell to tingling life.

Her gaze flew to meet his and a look she couldn't quite decipher flashed briefly in the depths of his gray eyes as the air around them thrummed with tension. She couldn't move, couldn't breathe, and when Reeve's head suddenly swooped down and his lips claimed hers, she was lost.

She'd forgotten how deliciously sweet, how devastatingly sensual and how damnably erotic a kiss could be; forgotten, too, how quickly desire could swamp the senses and drive common sense and good intentions out the window.

Her brain was telling her to pull away, to break the kiss, to stop the foolishness, but her body wasn't listening, aroused in no small measure by the taste of him, the scent of him and the feel of his rock-hard body pressed against hers.

At every point of contact, her skin felt as if it were on fire, and as his mouth ravaged hers, the ache steadily spreading through her began to escalate until she thought she might faint from wanting him.

Reeve couldn't seem to get enough. She tasted of a nectar more potent than any elixir, igniting a desire he hadn't felt in a long time. He'd always prided himself on being a man who seldom, if ever, lost control, but with a speed that stunned him, he found himself teetering helplessly on the edge of reason.

All at once, from the deep recesses of his memory, came the realization that this was exactly how it had been between them that June night so long ago when he'd made love to Shay in the secluded little sandy alcove between the Twin Rocks.

He hadn't meant for things to get out of hand that hot summer's night, hadn't planned to make love to her, but for the first time in his life, in the wake of the explosion of need that had erupted between them, his control had completely unraveled.

And it was happening again!

Shay was riding a wave of pure sensation, a wave that threatened at any second to drag her under and keep her there. She didn't care. She knew from the moment she'd set eyes on him again, she'd yearned for this, craved it. And as Reeve continued his tender assault, his tongue making deep forays into her mouth to tease and tempt, she responded with a wantonness only his kisses could incite, a wantonness he aroused with startling swiftness, a wantonness that ten years ago had changed the course of her life.

What was there about this man that affected her so deeply? She'd never been able to completely understand the feelings Reeve ignited in her. And she'd foolishly believed ten years ago that he'd felt something for her, too.

But she'd been wrong. Stupidly, naively wrong. Because he'd walked away without a backward glance and she had no reason to believe he wouldn't do the same again.

A moan of protest rumbled deep in her throat. Hadn't she vowed never again to let her heart rule her head? Hadn't she learned her lesson?

With a suddenness that surprised them both, Shay broke free of Reeve's embrace. 'No . . . not this . . . not again . . . ' She stepped back into the corridor, her body shaking, her heart hammering, her blood sizzling with need.

Reeve stared at her, his breath

ragged. 'Shay . . . forgive me. I should never have . . . ' He stumbled to a halt and dragged a trembling hand through his hair, all the while struggling to control emotions gone disastrously awry.

She hugged herself in a vain effort to ease the empty ache in her arms and in her heart. She heard regret as well as sadness in his voice and pain sliced through her. Without another word, she hurried down the hall to her own room and closed the door.

Reeve stood in the darkened hallway for several long minutes, taking deep steadying breaths waiting for his heart to stop pounding. Slowly, he made his way upstairs to his room and once inside leaned against the door waiting for his blood to cool.

He drew another deep breath, only to discover that Shay's scent, a mixture of summer flowers and wild roses lingered on him, and he knew as he ran his tongue over his lips that he'd tasted again the raging need, the urgent desire, both his and hers.

With a sigh, he crossed to the bed and sank onto it. Resting his elbows on his thighs, he lowered his head into his hands, while his mind kept replaying the electrifying kiss they'd shared, a kiss that should never have happened, a kiss that had stirred up old memories, memories he'd buried deep in his heart. He groaned and, rolling onto his back, lay down on the bed and stared up at the ceiling. Slowly, inevitably, his mind drifted back to that unforgettable night so long ago.

The reason he'd come back to Stuart's Cove that weekend had been to spend time with his father and say his farewells to old friends and neighbors before heading off to New York.

While he'd known his father had been proud of what he'd accomplished, Reeve had also known that Charles Walker had been disappointed that his son had chosen to complete his residency on the other side of the country.

As for Reeve, he'd wanted to get as far away as possible from the small coastal resort of Stuart's Cove. He'd had a yen to spread his wings, to explore life a little, take a bite out of the Big Apple.

His friendship with Jason Longford, fellow medical student and Louise's older brother, had helped sow the seeds of his discontent, and after meeting Jason's father, an eminent New York surgeon, the door of opportunity had opened and he'd stepped eagerly through it.

On that last weekend in Stuart's Cove, Reeve had had dinner with his father at their favorite seafood restaurant and throughout the meal had noticed a number of high school kids wearing formal dress, eating in the restaurant. He'd realized that it was the night of the high school graduation dance and remembered, too, that Shay would be one of the graduates.

He hadn't yet had a chance to see Shay or talk to her, and when his father had suddenly been called away on an emergency, Reeve decided to make his way to the gymnasium.

The three sets of double doors at the rear of the building had been opened to allow a cooling breeze to flow through. Reeve stood for a time in the doorway, listening to the rock band playing on stage, scanning the faces of the couples dancing to the music, in search of Shay.

He'd expected to find her wrapped in the arms of one of the handsome young men in her graduating class, but when he finally caught sight of her, she was alone, leaning against one of the pillars, looking incredibly beautiful in a dress the color of sapphires.

Ignoring the warning bells ringing in his head, he'd walked toward her through the couples crowding the floor, drawn by an invisible force, a force he'd been arrogantly confident he could control. He couldn't have been more wrong.

When he saw a look of excitement dance in her blue eyes, a brand-new emotion, one he hadn't recognized, snuck in under his guard, sending the blood pounding through his veins and a need clawing at his throat.

'May I have this dance?' he asked.

Without a word, she'd moved into his arms, fitting her body to his as if they were two halves of a whole. At the contact, he remembered the jolt of awareness that had rocked him like a tremor from an earthquake, sending his pulse into overdrive. He'd felt her breath sigh out against his cheek and felt, too, the sudden acceleration of her heartbeat, a beat that almost matched his own.

As their bodies moved in sensual rhythm to the music, he'd tried to tell himself that he would leave after one dance, just as he'd done on the night of her birthday. But when the last strains of the love song faded, he had been unwilling to relinquish his hold on her, aroused by her exotic scent and intoxicated by the feel of her bare skin beneath his fingers.

When the music changed to a faster rhythm, he'd felt a sharp tug of disappointment at having to release her. 'I'd better go. I just came by to say goodbye.' Silently, he berated himself for crashing the party, a party he should have stayed away from.

But ever since Christmas Eve, the night of Shay's birthday, he hadn't been able to get her out of his mind. If he'd been honest, he would have admitted to himself that he hadn't come back to Stuart's Cove just to say his farewells to his father, he'd come back to prove a point, to prove to himself that his feelings for Shay hadn't undergone any change, that what he felt for her was what he'd always felt, brotherly affection.

'Goodbye?' she said, a hint of breathlessness in her voice.

'I'm leaving for New York in a few days. I'm finishing my residency at a hospital there,' he explained.

'Oh . . . I see,' Shay replied. 'Will you write to me, Reeve?' she asked, her tone eager, her eyes wide. He'd written to her sporadically through college and had enjoyed receiving her newsy letters in return.

'I'm not sure I'll have time,' he answered truthfully, determined to cut all ties, to make a clean break. 'What about you? What are your plans now that you've graduated?'

'I don't know. I haven't decided,' Shay said. 'Listen, this isn't really my scene. Are you on your way home, by any chance? Would you mind dropping me off?'

'I came into town with my father, but he got called away,' Reeve said. 'I thought I'd just walk back.'

'Fine. I'll keep you company,' she instantly offered.

'You're not exactly wearing the right shoes for a walk in the country,' he said teasingly, glancing down at her high-heeled shoes, the same color as her dress.

'When have you ever known that to stop me?' she retorted.

Reeve laughed. He should have told

her he wasn't going home, told her anything to make her stay, but foolishly he'd thought there would be little harm in walking home with her.

And he might have been right if Shay hadn't suggested they take the shortcut behind the marina to the path leading to the Twin Rocks. He doubted he'd ever forget how she looked trekking barefoot over the rocks, wearing a gorgeous satin low-cut party dress, high heels in one hand, torn stockings in the other.

When they'd reached the sheltered sandy alcove where the Twin Rocks met and overlapped, they'd stopped for a rest and Reeve had gallantly removed his sports jacket, spreading it on the sand for her to sit on.

Midnight came and went as they sat side by side on the sand listening to the sound of the ocean gently lapping against the shore. Above them, the sky was aglow with a trillion bright stars and the moon hung over the water, its reflection dancing on the waves.

Wanting to fill the silence, Reeve had begun talking about his move to New York, about his ambition to find a permanent job in a big-city hospital and about the job opportunities he felt confident would come his way as a result of the move.

Shay had been silent throughout and when he finished, she'd turned to him. 'Sounds like you have your life all mapped out,' she said. 'I wish you everything you wish for yourself, Reeve, but before you leave, would you kiss me goodbye? For old time's sake?'

He'd darted a look at her, needing to see the expression in her eyes, but her face was streaked with moonlight and her eyes were concealed by the shadowed darkness of the alcove.

'Sure,' he'd replied more calmly than he felt. ''A kiss is just a kiss . . . ' Isn't that what Humphrey Bogart said in *Casablanca*? Or was it Ingrid Bergman who said it?'

Shay made no reply, and he wondered for a moment as he leaned toward her, if he was hallucinating, if she was really only a figment of his imagination.

She was all too real. Her lips, as cool and tangy as the ocean, tasted of moonlight and magic and something more, something sweeter, darker, deeper.

She sighed into his mouth and his mind blurred for just an instant with astonished pleasure as desire began to curl its powerful fist deep inside him until he was compelled to touch her, once again needing reassurance that she wasn't just a dream.

Her skin quivered beneath his fingers and he urged her closer, deepening the kiss, delving into the moist recesses of her mouth as a need more powerful than anything he'd ever known before, swept through him with lightning speed and staggering force.

As their tongues entwined in an erotic dance, Shay's wild and wanton response soon shattered what little control he had left, leaving his body a mass of aching need, a need only she could appease.

When she tugged his shirt free from the waistband of his trousers and her hands skimmed across his back, she blazed a trail of fire that sent his blood pressure soaring.

With only the moon as witness, they were soon lying naked on the cool sand and it was as Reeve drew her body against his that sanity returned, jolting him back to earth.

He stilled her questing hand as it caressed a spot somewhere near his heart. 'I must be insane. Do you have any idea what you're doing to me?' His voice was husky with suppressed emotion. 'Shay, we have to stop . . . now. I can't protect you . . . '

She gazed up at him, her eyes a silvery blue in the moonlight. 'I don't want you to stop,' she murmured throatily. Tugging her hand free, she reached up to run her fingers through his hair, drawing him closer. 'It's all right, Reeve, you don't have to worry.

I'm on the Pill,' she told him, and before he could form a reply, she closed the gap between them and covered his mouth with hers.

★ ★ ★

Reeve was rudely awakened Sunday morning by his daughter jumping onto his bed. He rolled over and tickled her and was immediately rewarded with chuckles of delight and a grin that melted his heart. Hugging Emma to him, he closed his eyes and sent up a silent prayer of thanks, telling himself it was only a matter of time before she spoke again.

When he opened his eyes, a small figure standing in the doorway of the adjoining rooms caught his attention. Mandy stood staring at them, a look of longing in her blue eyes.

'Hey, Mandy,' Reeve greeted her with a smile. 'Thanks for helping your mom look after Emma for me last night. It was really nice of you to let her sleep in your bed.'

'That's okay. We had fun. Didn't we, Emma?' Mandy said as her cheeks turned a lovely shade of pink.

Reeve turned to his daughter and held his breath. But Emma only nodded and he had to bite back the sigh of disappointment that threatened to escape.

Reaching over to retrieve his watch from the bedside table, Reeve was surprised to note that it was almost ten-thirty. 'Look at the time! I guess I forgot to set my alarm. You two better scram so I can get showered and dressed.'

'Are you going to the clinic today?' Mandy asked.

'No,' he replied. 'This is my day off. One of the doctors from the hospital in Fernhaven takes over on Sundays. So, what would you two like to do this afternoon?'

'How about a picnic on the beach?' Mandy was quick to respond.

'Emma?' Reeve glanced at his daughter. 'Would you like to go on a picnic?'

178

Emma nodded, her eyes twinkling with excitement.

Reeve touched a finger to Emma's nose. 'Sounds like a great idea to me, too,' he said. 'But maybe you should check with your mother, Mandy.'

'Okay' came the reply. 'Come on, Emma. Let's go ask her.'

Emma planted a quick kiss on Reeve's cheek before hopping off his bed and running to catch up with Mandy.

Reeve smiled to himself as he relaxed against the pillows, marveling at the changes that had taken place in his daughter since they'd arrived in Stuart's Cove a week ago. The child psychologist had been right. The complete change of environment he'd recommended had indeed had a positive effect on Emma.

The fact that she'd spoken was a tremendous relief to him and a giant leap forward for her. But silently, Reeve acknowledged that Mandy and Shay had played significant roles in Emma's transformation from the withdrawn, anxious child, to the smiling, happy girl who'd just left his bedroom.

Reeve found his thoughts shifting to Shay, to the kiss they'd shared last night, and his subsequent trip down memory lane. For most of the night, his dreams had been haunted by those memories of Shay and of a night he'd never been able to forget.

He'd made love to her a second time just as dawn was breaking. He'd awakened her with a tender kiss, a kiss that had quickly escalated into a fiery need. Afterward, as they'd walked the remaining distance home, he hadn't known what to say, or how to express the feelings waging a war within him.

When he'd left Shay outside the inn that morning, he'd promised her he would call, but he'd been at the airport, ready to board his flight back to Vancouver before he'd finally found the courage to make the call. Coward that he was, he'd been relieved when Isabel O'Brien had answered the phone and he hadn't had to talk to Shay.

He wasn't at all proud of how he'd behaved that night, filled with remorse and guilt at having neither the strength nor the willpower to control the desire she had aroused in him.

Two days later, he'd flown to New York where he'd pushed thoughts of Shay to the back of his mind, telling himself over and over that he'd worked long and hard for this chance, and he'd be a fool to turn his back on it, that what he'd shared with Shay had been simply a night of summer madness.

Besides, he silently rationalized as he pushed the covers aside and rose from the bed, Shay had obviously become involved with another man soon after their encounter. She had a daughter to prove it.

As he stood under the shower, Reeve found his thoughts turning to the man who'd been Shay's lover. She must have met him in Europe, he reasoned. But the relationship obviously hadn't worked out, and after the breakdown of his own marriage he could sympathize with both parties.

Mandy had to be about eight or a little older, and Reeve wondered, not for the first time, why Shay was so averse to talking about the child's father. Had she left France in order to get away from him? Or could it be that the reason she was unwilling to talk about Mandy's father was that she still had unresolved feelings for the man?

As Reeve turned off the shower and reached for a towel, he was surprised to discover that this thought irritated him more than he was willing to admit.

⋆   ⋆   ⋆

'Can we have a picnic on the beach this afternoon?' Mandy asked. 'Emma's dad doesn't have to go to the clinic today, and he thinks a picnic is a good idea,' Mandy said.

Shay, who'd been standing at the sink washing romaine lettuce, shook the moisture from her hands and turned to look at her daughter. Both children stood gazing up at her with pleading expressions on their round faces and in their cornflower blue eyes.

'Well . . . I suppose,' she began, not without reluctance, simply because the thought of spending the afternoon in Reeve's company sent a shiver of alarm as well as anticipation chasing up her spine.

'Does that mean yes?' Mandy asked.

'Yes,' Shay answered and was rewarded with a smile from both girls. 'So, your father's awake now, is he?' she asked, smiling encouragingly at Emma, hoping for a verbal reply.

'Yeah, Reeve's awake,' Mandy promptly replied. 'He'll be downstairs in a little while. He's taking a shower first.'

Shay felt her pulse pick up speed at the thought of having to face Reeve for the first time since the blistering kiss they'd shared. She'd spent a restless night plagued by the memories his kiss had aroused, memories of another night so long ago.

Shay was determined Reeve would never know the truth, or know just how much his kiss, his very presence, affected her.

The fact that the girls were in the kitchen when he appeared helped defuse Shay's inner tension. But there was no ignoring the tremor that raced along her flesh at the sight of him.

Dressed in a pair of khaki shorts and a sage green short-sleeved shirt unbuttoned to reveal a sprinkling of dark chest hairs, he looked the epitome of every woman's fantasy lover, with his dark mahogany hair still wet from the shower and his clean-shaven jaw begging to be stroked.

If she'd hoped, in some quiet corner of her heart, that Reeve might give some indication that the kiss they'd shared had affected him at all, she was doomed to disappointment, and his easy smile and nonchalant manner as he ate his breakfast gave nothing away.

And another disappointment she had to face was the fact that since putting up the Vacancy sign the day before, she'd had no response whatsoever. Even the advertisements she'd placed in various newspapers hadn't generated even as much as a telephone call.

While she kept telling herself it was early days yet and she was probably overanxious about making a success of the inn, she had hoped to attract at least a few visitors over the weekend.

'What's the word on the picnic?' Reeve asked as Shay cleared away his breakfast dishes.

'Sounds like fun,' Shay replied, keeping her tone light. 'But I think we should wait until two o'clock or later before we head to the beach. If we go earlier, the sun is much too hot, and we're liable to get sunburned, even wearing sunscreen.'

'Your mother's right,' Reeve acknowledged. 'What shall we do in the meantime, girls? I know. What about your tree house, Mandy? Do you still want to put a roof on it?'

'Yes . . . but . . . ' Mandy glanced at

her mother for approval.

'Why don't we go and take some measurements and see how much wood it would need?' Reeve said. 'As long as it's all right with your mother, of course,' he went on, having noted the brief exchange between mother and daughter.

'Mom?' Mandy flashed her mother a pleading look.

Shay felt like a rabbit trapped in the headlights of a car as three sets of eyes focused on her, waiting for her answer. 'I don't suppose it would do any harm to measure,' she said after a long moment, and caught the glint of amusement dancing in the depths of Reeve's gray eyes.

'Great! Let's do that right now,' Reeve suggested, rising from the table. 'Come on, kids. At least we'll be in the shade.'

Shay watched as the children followed Reeve from the kitchen. Much as she felt she should be annoyed at him for wanting to help Mandy put a roof on the tree house, she couldn't seem to summon up any feelings of anger.

The fact that Reeve hadn't suggested taking Emma off on her own for the day, but was making a point of including Mandy in their activities, touched her deeply and brought those old feelings of guilt rushing to the surface.

It didn't help that Mandy obviously openly adored the man who was her father, and not for the first time since his return to Stuart's Cove, Shay found herself wondering just how he would react if he was to learn the truth.

* * *

It was past two o'clock before the four of them began to make their way along the path leading down to the beach. A few white clouds floated lazily in the blue sky, and a cooling breeze came from the water to whisper through the old arbutus trees that lined the top of the path.

Reeve carried the picnic basket, while Shay carried a beach umbrella and blanket as well as a small canvas bag with sunscreen, sunglasses, a book and a few sundries. Having spent some time putting sunscreen on each other, the girls, already in their bathing suits, raced on ahead, chasing after the multicolored beach ball Mandy had unearthed from her closet.

Before leaving the inn, Shay had left a note pinned to the front door, telling any prospective bed-and-breakfast customer where they could be found. A small number of suntanners and picnickers occupied various spots along the stretch of sand, all enjoying the warm summer sunshine.

After helping Shay spread out the blanket and put up the umbrella, Reeve challenged the girls to a game of catch. Shay declined his invitation to join in, giving the excuse that she'd rather sit and read.

Moments later, when Reeve shrugged off his shirt, Shay felt her stomach muscles tense at the sight of his broad tanned back. She turned away, rummaging in her canvas bag in search of her sunglasses and book.

When she heard the sound of the zipper on Reeve's shorts being lowered, she froze and her breath caught in her throat as a ripple of sensation washed over her. From beneath lowered lashes, Shay dared to peek at Reeve as he moved off to join the girls waiting for him near the edge of the water.

Her heart somersaulted inside her chest as she drank in the long lean lines of his tanned body. Lazily now, she let her gaze slide appreciatively up his muscular legs and thighs, to his firm buttocks encased in a turquoise bathing suit and on up his back to take in the breadth and width of his shoulders.

Suddenly, her fingers itched to touch him, to explore the muscled contours, to feel again the silky smoothness of his skin. Dropping her gaze, she slowly released the breath she hadn't known she'd been holding, annoyed at the direction her thoughts had taken.

Slipping on her sunglasses, she rolled onto her stomach and propped the paperback novel in front of her, but her mind refused to focus on the words, her eyes continually darting to where Reeve ran splashing into the water with a child clinging to each of his hands.

Shay's eyes filled with tears as she watched Reeve with his daughters. He was the kind of father every child deserved, caring, loving, supportive and most important, fun to be with.

There had been times during the past ten years when she had been pursued by several handsome, eligible men, only one of whom she'd liked. For the most part, she'd found them sorely lacking in patience and a sense of fun, both necessary attributes, especially when it came to dealing with children.

When at age four Mandy began asking questions about her father, Shay had kept her answers short and as truthful as possible. And after a while, Mandy had come to accept Shay's explanation that her father had loved someone else and married someone else. But what Shay had noticed had been Mandy's tendency to be wary and more reserved around men, especially men who showed an interest in her mother.

While Reeve hadn't shown any such interest in Shay, Mandy's usual reserve didn't seem to apply where he was concerned, and Shay couldn't help wondering if the reason for the easy rapport they shared was because of their blood ties.

Feeling suddenly hot, Shay rose from the blanket and, slipping off her pink and white terry-towel cover-up, padded down the sand to the water. She waved to Reeve and the girls as she waded into the water and moments later dived beneath one of the larger waves.

The silky coolness of the water closed over her like a lover's caress. Holding her breath, she slowly stroked away from the shore, breaking the surface a short time later to take a breath before rolling over onto her back.

She closed her eyes against the sun's brightness and, kicking her feet, floated gently out to sea, trying with difficulty to clear her mind. Suddenly, she felt something brush past her and her eyes flew open in time to see Reeve pop up beside her.

At the sight of him, Shay's heart began to beat a thunderous tattoo against her breast and she had to quickly tread water in order to stay afloat. 'What are you doing here?' Annoyance echoed through her voice. 'Where are the children?'

'On the beach,' Reeve replied as he waved in their direction.

Shay glanced over her shoulder and saw both girls waving from the edge of the water. She waved back.

'I came out because Mandy looked a little worried when you didn't surface right away,' Reeve explained. 'I guess she hasn't seen you swimming out here before.'

'No, she hasn't' was all Shay could

say. This was the first time since her return to Stuart's Cove that she'd been afforded the opportunity to indulge in a quiet swim on her own.

'I reminded Mandy that we both grew up here, both learned to swim here and that you're a very strong swimmer,' Reeve went on.

'Thanks,' Shay replied.

'But that doesn't mean you shouldn't forget how dangerous these waters can be at times, especially if you go out too far,' Reeve warned, his gray gaze intent on hers.

'I'll try to remember that,' Shay said, knowing he was right. With quick powerful strokes, she turned and began to swim back to shore, thinking that while the water could indeed be a danger, Reeve and the feelings he could so easily arouse in her were infinitely more hazardous to her peace of mind.

7

Shay walked out of the water, with Reeve close behind. Mandy came running toward her, a worried expression clouding her small features.

'Mommy! I thought you'd drowned,' Mandy blurted out, obviously close to tears.

Shay quickly crouched to her daughter's level, and put her arms around the child, hugging her tightly, silently berating herself for having frightened her. 'Sweetheart, I'm sorry if I scared you,' Shay said, grateful when Reeve moved to divert Emma's attention, picking up his daughter and carrying her up the beach.

'You dived under, and I couldn't see you,' Mandy said with a hiccup, still clinging to Shay, reminding her that while her daughter liked to give the impression she was an independent,

194

confident outgoing child, there were times when she was just a little girl needing her mother's love and reassurance.

'I'm sorry. Mommy wasn't thinking straight.'

She'd been too preoccupied with the emotions Reeve's near-naked body had aroused in her to stop and think about how it would look to Mandy to see her walk into the ocean and disappear under the swell of a wave for ten or twenty seconds.

'Reeve said you used to swim out there every summer,' Mandy said, pulling back to look into her mother's eyes.

'That's right,' Shay replied. 'Don't you remember the stories Aunt Izzy told you about how she taught me to swim right here in the cove?'

Mandy nodded as she absently brushed a stray tear from her cheek. 'I forgot,' she said.

'Hey. That's okay,' Shay replied.

'Can you teach me how to swim?' Mandy asked.

'I could,' Shay said. 'But I think it would be better if I enrolled you in some swimming lessons at the pool in the recreation center. That way, you'd learn from a real instructor. What do you say?'

'When?' Mandy asked.

'I'll call the center later and find out when the next session starts,' Shay offered.

'Thanks, Mom.' Mandy hugged Shay.

Shay smiled and kissed Mandy's cheek. 'Come on. We'd better catch up with Reeve and Emma. We don't want them eating all the goodies we brought for the picnic, do we?' she teased.

'No way!' Mandy announced, and spinning around, she broke into a run, her anxiety obviously gone, much to Shay's relief.

Emma, Reeve and Mandy were seated on the blanket when Shay joined them. 'All right. Who wants lemonade?' she asked as she accepted the towel Reeve held out for her. 'Thanks,' she murmured and wiped the remaining moisture from her face and neck, aware all the while of Reeve watching her, a look that sent a delicious tremor racing through her.

'I do! I do!' Mandy replied. 'And Emma does, too,' she quickly added.

'You two get out the plastic cups, and I'll pour.' Reeve directed his comment to the girls, managing to drag his gaze away from Shay to the picnic hamper. Shay's one-piece navy-and-white-striped bathing suit fit like a glove, leaving little to his imagination, and Reeve was finding the sight of Shay's silky-smooth, lightly tanned skin much too distracting for his peace of mind.

'Are we going to have our picnic now?' Mandy asked, holding out a plastic cup for her mother.

'By all means, let's eat,' Shay responded. Dropping onto the blanket, she tried to move into the shade of the umbrella. 'There's cold chicken, green salad, buns and potato chips. And for dessert, we have homemade carrot cake. Help yourselves.'

Mandy, her earlier apprehension clearly forgotten, handed out paper plates and forks and, with her father's and Emma's help, soon had everything set out on the blanket. Shay gently rubbed the ends of her hair with the towel, wishing she'd had the forethought to tuck her hairbrush into the canvas bag.

When the picnic was finished, Reeve helped Shay put the leftovers back into their respective containers, while the children ran to the water's edge to rinse the stickiness from their hands.

'Mandy seems to have gotten over her scare,' Reeve said as he closed the lid of the picnic hamper.

'Yes, thank goodness,' Shay replied with heartfelt emotion. 'She asked me to teach her how to swim, and I told her I'd see about enrolling her in some lessons.'

'Good idea.' Reeve stretched his long tanned legs and lay back on the blanket.

'I haven't had an opportunity to

swim on my own since coming back here, and I never leave Mandy on the beach by herself. I knew she was with you and I wasn't thinking,' Shay said.

'Thanks,' Reeve said after a brief silence. 'The fact that you trust me to look after Mandy means a great deal to me. I only wish Louise had had that much faith in me when Emma was born, but she insisted on doing everything herself almost to the point of exclusion.'

Shay heard the bitter note in his voice and a pain squeezed her heart. 'Of course I trust you. You're her — ' Abruptly, she snapped her mouth closed, astonished and appalled at what she'd been about to say. Reeve threw her a puzzled frown and Shay felt her heart skip a beat in panic.

'I'm her what?' Reeve asked, rolling onto his side and propping his head on his hand. He sounded amused and just a little curious, and Shay tried with difficulty to appear casual and uncon-cerned.

'Ah . . . I was going to say that you're practically her uncle,' she improvised, praying silently that he would accept her explanation and not probe further.

Avoiding his gaze, she pulled her canvas bag toward her, all the while thinking that she'd narrowly averted a disaster. She'd been about to say, 'You're her father,' a slip of the tongue that would have cost her dearly.

Intent on keeping her gaze away from Reeve's, she rummaged inside the bag and moments later brought out a bottle of sunscreen. Pretending a nonchalance she was far from feeling, she squeezed some of the cream onto her hands and began to smooth it over her face and arms.

'Here, let me put some of that on your back for you,' Reeve offered, and before Shay could form a refusal, he shifted to a sitting position and lifted the bottle from her unresisting fingers.

The second he touched her, a ribbon of sensation spiraled down her spine and through her limbs. Had she been standing, Shay knew without a shadow of a doubt that her legs would have buckled under her. As it was, her breath caught in her throat and it was all she could do to make her lungs continue to function.

His fingers were warm and decidedly erotic as he smoothed the cream on her back with slow seductive strokes. Her blood began to pound, her skin to vibrate, as his hands worked their magic, arousing every nerve, every cell to tingling life. As her eyelids fluttered closed in sweet surrender, she had to bite down on the inner softness of her mouth to stop the moan of longing suddenly hovering on her lips.

Her skin was like rose petals, smooth and fragrant, and as Reeve gently massaged the curve of her shoulder, he had to fight the urge to push aside the silky swath of her sundried hair and cover her neck with wet kisses.

He leaned closer and drew in a deep breath. Along with it came the tangy scent of the ocean as well as a more evocative scent, a scent that was hers alone, tantalizingly sexy and disturbingly arousing.

Don't stop! Please don't stop! Shay's eyes flew open in alarm as she wondered for a heart-stopping moment if she'd spoken the words aloud. But when Reeve made no comment and continued his exquisite brand of torture, his hand trailing a path to the edge of her bathing suit and back up again. Shay forced herself to breathe normally.

'Mommy!' Mandy's shout, like the sudden squawk of a sea gull, sliced through the air, capturing her attention and stilling Reeve's hand. Glancing at the children near the water's edge, she could see both Mandy and Emma beckoning to her. 'Quick! Come and see what we found!' Mandy urged.

Reeve reacted first, hopping to his feet with one deft movement. 'I'll go,' he said.

'Wait! I'll come, too,' Shay responded, starting to get up.

Reeve instantly offered his hand and

after the briefest of hesitations, Shay reached out and grasped it. As his warm fingers folded around hers, she felt a quick jolt to her system, which sent a flurry of emotion rippling through her.

Once on her feet, she bravely met his gaze. Her heart tumbled drunkenly against her ribs as a look she'd never seen there before, a sad kind of yearning, flashed briefly in his eyes, then was gone.

'Mom!' Mandy's more urgent yell effectively broke the silence and the tension arcing between them. Reeve released her and they turned and hurried to where the children waited.

Mandy and Emma's discovery turned out to be a beautiful conch shell. Its tip was all that could be seen poking out of the wet sand, and unable to pull it free, Mandy had called for assistance. Reeve knelt and, like an archaeologist uncovering an ancient ruin, carefully dug and scraped the sand away until the entire shell was revealed.

'Wow!' Mandy said, eyes wide with wonder as Reeve lifted it free. After gently shaking the sand from it, he walked into the water and rinsed the remaining grains of sand from the brown, gold and white shell.

'Girls, you've found a treasure here,' Reeve said. 'And it's in near-perfect condition.'

'It's so beautiful,' Mandy said, taking it from Reeve's outstretched hand. She turned to Emma. 'Look, Emma. Isn't it neat? And I bet if you put it up to your ear, you'll hear the ocean. Won't she, Mommy?' Mandy asked, flashing her mother a bright smile.

'Try it,' Shay suggested, delighted by the joy she could see in the faces of both girls.

Mandy held the shell to Emma's ear, and Shay watched Emma's blue eyes widen in astonished pleasure as she listened to the magic of the shell.

'It's yours to keep, Emma. You found it,' Mandy said decisively, without the slightest hint of envy or resentment.

At Mandy's words, Emma's mouth opened in surprise and her gaze flew to her father's face, clearly searching for approval as well as confirmation.

'That's very generous of you, Mandy,' Reeve said, moved immeasurably by the child's gesture.

'Emma spotted it. It's hers,' Mandy reiterated, obviously a believer of the adage, 'Finders keepers.' 'And when she goes back to New York, she'll have something to remind her of the time she spent here with us,' Mandy added, giving her half sister a warm smile.

Shay, her heart bursting with pride at her daughter's unselfish act, watched as Emma's eyes, so like Mandy's, filled with tears.

All at once, Emma opened her mouth as if she was about to speak.

Shay felt her heart leap into her throat and her gaze flew to meet Reeve's in time to see a look of anticipation and hope register in his eyes. But after several breathless seconds, Emma seemed to change her mind and threw her arms around Mandy, giving her half sister a hug.

As Reeve watched the children, the disappointment tugging at him quickly evaporated, replaced by a feeling of warmth. That the children had formed a strong, almost sisterly, bond was obvious. Shifting his gaze, Reeve noted the look of pride and love glowing in Shay's blue eyes as she, too, watched the girls embrace.

But a moment later, when Shay's glance collided with his, Reeve was surprised to see guilt flash briefly in their depths before she dropped her gaze from his.

Puzzled, Reeve wondered if he'd been mistaken. What could Shay have to feel guilty about?

★   ★   ★

'After all the fun and excitement Emma had today, I thought she would fall asleep the moment her head hit the pillow,' Reeve commented when he rejoined Shay in the kitchen later that evening.

'Mandy was a little hyper tonight, too,' Shay said. 'Maybe they both got a little too much sun.' She turned from the fridge, the pitcher of lemonade in her hand, and filled the two glasses sitting on the counter.

'Emma insisted on putting the shell on her bedside table,' Reeve went on. 'I think she would have slept with it under her pillow, if I'd let her.' He laughed softly and shook his head.

'That shell is quite a rare find,' Shay said as she handed him a glass of lemonade. 'I recall one of Aunt Izzy's visitors finding a similar one. But that was years ago.'

'Thanks.' Reeve lifted the glass in salute. 'I doubt I'll ever forget the look on Emma's face when Mandy told her the shell was hers to keep,' he added as he pulled out a kitchen chair and sat down. 'Oh. Hello there, Patches,' he added as the kitten jumped from one of the other chairs into his lap.

'You can put her in her box if she's bothering you,' Shay told him.

'She's all right,' Reeve replied, absently stroking the kitten with one hand. He smiled as she curled up contentedly on his lap. 'I was so sure Emma was going to speak this afternoon, to thank Mandy for the shell.' Disappointment echoed through his voice.

Shay nodded. 'I thought so, too,' she agreed, recalling those fleeting moments of tension before Emma had hugged her half sister instead.

'I'm beginning to think I only imagined her calling out to me yesterday.' Reeve's tone was dipped in despair.

'You didn't imagine it,' Shay was quick to assure him as she sat down in the chair Patches had just vacated. 'Don't forget how far she's come already,' she reminded him. 'She's smiling all the time now.'

'You're right,' Reeve agreed. 'And it's wonderful to see the change in her. She seems much happier, much more at peace, somehow.'

'And any day now, when she's ready, she'll just start talking, and there'll be no turning back,' she predicted, feeling reasonably sure that once Emma's confidence was totally restored, once she realized her father loved her regardless of whether she spoke or not, she would emerge from her silent world.

'I sincerely hope you're right,' Reeve said with more confidence than he felt. He flashed Shay a smile. 'This is certainly a reversal of roles.' He took a large sip of lemonade.

'What do you mean?' Shay asked, frowning.

'Me getting advice from you,' he replied as he set the glass on the table. 'If my memory serves me, you were the one always bending my ear about a problem you had at school, or an argument you had with your aunt,' Reeve said. 'Don't you remember? You even asked me once how to go about getting a date.' Humor laced his tone.

'You're fudging the truth a little there,' Shay challenged. 'I simply wanted to know whether you thought any boy would ever ask me out,' she corrected, recalling clearly the conversation he was talking about.

'And I told you that guys would be lining up at your door,' Reeve countered. 'You didn't believe me at the time. But I was right, wasn't I?' A teasing grin tugged at the corners of his mouth.

'That was a long time ago,' Shay responded, feeling her face grow warm under his smiling scrutiny. He had been right about boys being interested in her, but she'd never felt as comfortable with any of those young men as she had with Reeve.

The first inkling she'd had that her friendship with Reeve had shifted to a new and different level had been on the night of her eighteenth birthday, when he'd danced with her. During those achingly tender moments when he'd held her close, he'd aroused her senses and awakened her sensuality, only to walk away and leave her confused and bewildered by the encounter.

She'd had to wait five long months to see him again, and on that starry night in June with only the moon and stars to bear witness, she'd finally faced the startling truth about her feelings for him.

With just one kiss, a kiss branded forever in her memory, he had sealed her fate and foolishly, naively, she'd poured everything into her response, believing with every fiber of her being that he had to feel the same about her. How else could he have made love to her?

'Shay. Shay . . . ?'

The deep rich timbre of Reeve's voice floated through the mist of her memories. 'What . . . ? Sorry.' Her throat was bone dry. Her voice husky with suppressed emotion. 'I was daydreaming,' she declared, silently chastising herself for allowing those painful memories to resurface. Lifting her glass of lemonade, she took several sips.

'From the look on your face, he must have been someone very special,' Reeve said softly.

Shay's heart did a cartwheel inside her chest. 'Who?'

'Whoever you were daydreaming about just then, that's who,' Reeve replied, finding it difficult to keep the irritation out of his voice, surprised to discover that the thought of Shay daydreaming about a man, *any* man, annoyed him immensely.

Shay met his gaze and wondered at the faint edge in his tone and the steely glint she could see in the depths of his eyes. She must be imagining things! Surely Reeve wasn't jealous? No. She dismissed the notion immediately and almost laughed out loud a moment later when she realized that if jealousy had indeed been what she'd heard in his voice, he was jealous of himself.

'Tell me, Reeve. Was New York

everything you hoped it would be?' she asked, suddenly needing to shift the focus of attention away from herself.

Reeve's hand suddenly stilled in the act of stroking the kitten and a thoughtful, rather sad expression flitted across his handsome features.

'New York was . . . New York is, big, bold, beautiful and at times brutal. But there's no place in the world quite like it,' he said.

Shay heard the genuine warmth and affection in his voice. 'So you like living there,' she stated.

'Yes, I do,' Reeve replied truthfully. 'Once I got over the initial awe of simply being in the Big Apple, I was amazed how quickly I began to feel at home. They say you either love it or hate it. I love it.'

'And your career? Has it gone exactly as you'd planned? Did you attain all the goals you set for yourself?' Shay asked, curious to learn how far his burning ambition had taken him.

Reeve's features creased into a frown.

'Yes, at least for the most part,' he answered after a lengthy pause. 'I've been lucky,' he added. After leaving Stuart's Cove ten years ago, he'd worked long and hard to gain acceptance and prove his worth in a field that was highly competitive. But after five years, he'd been offered a permanent place on the hospital's staff and since then he'd been working tirelessly toward his ultimate goal, becoming head of the Trauma Unit.

'I doubt luck had anything to do with it,' Shay said, cutting through his musings. 'It's more than likely you worked your butt off and left the rest of the field at the starting gate.'

Reeve lifted his gaze to meet hers, surprised that she'd homed in on the truth with such speed and accuracy. But then, he shouldn't really be surprised, she'd known him almost better than he'd known himself.

He smiled. 'And luck is still shining on me,' Reeve said. 'Before Emma and I left New York, I was offered the job of head of the Trauma Unit at Manhattan Metro.'

'That's terrific. Congratulations,' Shay said with forced brightness, wondering why his announcement should cause a pain to twist in her heart.

'Thank you,' Reeve responded, refraining from adding that he hadn't, as yet, accepted the position. When Dr. Clayton, the hospital's chief of operations, had dropped into Reeve's office the day before he and Emma left New York, Reeve had assumed he'd come to exchange pleasantries.

But Russell Clayton had proceeded to inform Reeve that the current unit head had decided to take early retirement and the board had authorized him to offer the post to Reeve, adding that he could give the hospital board an answer on his return.

On the drive back to his apartment, Reeve had told himself that Emma's accident and his preoccupation with her condition was undoubtedly the reason he hadn't immediately accepted the post, the position he'd been working toward for the past two years.

But while he knew he was more than qualified and capable of running the unit, he also knew that as its head, his responsibilities would double and ultimately result in more working hours for him and less time with Emma.

Emma was his responsibility, totally and completely, and she wasn't a responsibility he took lightly. Her happiness and well-being were of the utmost importance, and having already missed a major portion of his daughter's life, thanks to the machinations and manipulations of his ex-wife, Reeve wasn't about to hand over Emma's care to someone else.

But that's exactly what he would have to do if he accepted the hospital board's offer. Could he in all conscience take on the job, knowing that his daughter would be the one to suffer?

'Reeve?' Shay's voice cut through his wandering thoughts and he blinked twice in order to refocus on her.

'Sorry, I was miles away,' he said.

Or at least wishing you were, thought Shay with a sigh, having for the past few minutes watched a range of emotions dance across his handsome face. Reeve's career was obviously on track and New York appeared to be the place he regarded as his home. Silently, Shay reminded herself that in two short weeks he and Emma would be returning to the Big Apple and their brief sojourn in Stuart's Cove would be nothing more than a memory.

'Would you like more lemonade?' she asked, rising from the chair.

Reeve smiled. 'No, thank you' came the reply. 'Patches, I hate to disturb you, but I have some paperwork that needs my attention.' Sliding his hand beneath the kitten, he lifted her from his lap.

'Ouch!' Reeve reacted with a start.

Undoubtedly startled by Reeve's unexpected move, Patches had made her displeasure known by digging her tiny but sharp claws into Reeve's hand and wrist.

'Are you all right?' Shay asked, moving closer. 'I'll take her,' she offered and managed to extricate the struggling kitten, setting her on the kitchen floor. 'Here, let me take a look,' Shay offered, knowing from experience just how painful a scratch from the kitten could be.

'I'm fine,' Reeve assured her, looking down at his hand.

'No, you're not. You're bleeding,' Shay told him noticing the spots of blood appearing on the inside of his wrist.

'Damn! It stings,' Reeve conceded, grimacing at the needle-sharp pinpricks of pain.

Shay reached out and grasped his hand with hers, intent on taking a closer look. At the contact, her heart skipped a beat as a tingling warmth she recognized all too readily began to slowly steal over her fingers and up her arm.

'You'll live,' she managed to say, keeping her head bent and her eyes averted, while tiny shivers of sensation danced across her nerve endings, leaving a trail of need in their wake.

'I'm not so sure about that.' Reeve's deep husky tone brought her head up and as their gazes collided, her breath locked in her throat and her senses veered madly off course when she saw the raw desire glowing like diamonds in the depths of his gray eyes.

Her heart began to trip against her ribs like a jackhammer. She couldn't move, mesmerized by the look in his eyes. The air was suffocating, the silence deafening as she stood waiting, hoping, aching, until his image blurred and his mouth crushed hers in a kiss that had her instantly trembling with desire.

His taste was dark and erotically male, and in the span of a heartbeat she was clinging to him as if she might never let go. His tongue danced and entwined with hers, taunting and teasing until her head was spinning and her blood was sizzling through her veins in dazzling excitement.

She wanted more. Her skin seemed to ache all over, longing to feel again the touch of his hands, to know again the mindless passion only he could arouse and to reach once more those dizzying heights.

What was there about this man that evoked such a startling and overwhelming response within her, a response that she'd never been able to control? She moaned softly, whether in protest or frustration she wasn't exactly sure.

Reeve heard the vulnerable sound vibrating in her throat and a tremor shook his body as his own need quickly escalated to a dangerous level. He kissed her harder, longer, deeper, trying somehow to appease the primitive hunger clutching at his insides and making him want to bury himself in her softness.

What was there about this woman that made him tremble like a leaf in the wind, who with just one kiss could shatter his control into a zillion tiny pieces?

'Mommy, I can't sleep. Can I have a drink of water?' Mandy's plaintive cry echoed down the hall and at the sound Shay felt as if someone had suddenly thrown ice-cold water over her.

Wrenching herself free of Reeve's arms, she backed away until she felt the edge of the counter. 'What am I doing?' The question, directed at herself, came out in a breathless whisper.

'Shay . . . ?' Reeve's voice was ragged, and it was all he could do not to haul her back into his arms.

'Don't . . . please,' Shay begged, fighting to calm her racing heart.

'Mom? Are you there?' This time, Mandy's tone held a hint of concern.

'Yes, sweetheart. I'm coming,' Shay called out. Turning her back on Reeve, she reached into the cupboard for a glass. As she filled the glass with water, she knew Reeve hadn't moved, knew by the tension shimmering through her that he was still there, staring at her.

She kept her back to him, silently praying he would leave. When she heard

221

his muffled curse, followed by the sound of his receding footsteps, Shay sagged against the counter with relief, almost dropping the glass of water in her hand.

She stood for several seconds waiting for her heartbeat to return to a more normal rhythm. Drawing a deep steadying breath, she berated herself for allowing the kiss to happen at all. She could have avoided it. Should have avoided it! But instead, she'd clung to him like a limpet to a rock, responding to his mouth's demands like a lovesick, sex-starved fool.

Ten years ago on a hot summer's night, she'd handed Reeve her heart only to have him trample it in his haste to leave town. At twenty-eight, she was older and much wiser, certainly wise enough not to want history to repeat itself. But as she headed down the hall to her daughter's room, Shay couldn't quite banish from her mind the feel of Reeve's mouth on hers or the fact that it felt so right to be in his arms.

8

It was late Monday afternoon when to Shay and the children's delight, her first bed-and-breakfast customers, Maggie and David Burnside from California, appeared on the doorstep.

The Burnsides stayed for two nights and had just driven off, when two young women from Washington State and a couple from Germany arrived in search of accommodations. Fritz and Marina Kruger spent the remainder of the week at the inn, using it as a central base from which to explore the area, while Amee and Becky stayed one night, promising to return at a future date.

As a result, Shay spent a busy week catering to her guests, but was glad of the extra work that helped to keep her thoughts away from Reeve. Fearful of a repeat of the kiss they'd shared, Shay made a point of trying to avoid being alone with him, and for the most part she succeeded.

Reeve's routine remained the same. After a day spent at the clinic, he would arrive back at the inn in time to help Shay and the children prepare their evening meal. After supper, he and the girls would walk down to the beach to play ball on the sand, or search for shells.

On Wednesday evening, Reeve, Emma and Mandy made a brief trip to his father's house to check on the renovations. While Reeve always issued an invitation to Shay to join them on these nightly outings, she politely declined and tried each time to ignore the puzzled expression which appeared in her daughter's eyes.

Having said goodbye to the German couple earlier that morning, it was almost noon on Saturday when Shay finally finished cleaning bedrooms and bathrooms. Mandy and Emma waited outside while Shay wrote a grocery list in preparation for the trip into town to the supermarket. As she gathered her purse and keys from the counter, the telephone rang.

'Shay? Is that you?' a voice asked.

'Alice! How lovely to hear from you,' Shay responded. 'How is Paris?'

'Paris is simply wonderful. It's everything you said it would be and more,' Alice replied with a heartfelt sigh. 'A beautiful and romantic city.'

'I gather you're having a good time,' Shay said, pleased that Alice and Charles were enjoying their honeymoon.

'We're having a fabulous time,' Alice assured her. 'How are you and Mandy, and Reeve and Emma doing?'

'Everyone's fine,' Shay replied.

'Charles wants to know how Reeve's managing at the clinic,' Alice said.

'As far as I know, things are running smoothly,' Shay reported.

'Charles was going to call Reeve there, but I suggested giving you a ring instead,' Alice said. 'What about the renovations? Do you know how they're coming along?'

'Reeve and the girls drove up to take a look a few nights ago and he said the work appeared to be going well,' she said. 'I believe your new bathroom is almost finished.'

'That's good to hear,' Alice said. 'We would have called sooner, but we've been so busy. Charles and I have taken every bus tour our hotel has had to offer, and in between, we've ventured out on our own. Today we rode the subway, I mean the metro, to the Louvre.'

Shay gave a sigh of envy. The last time she'd wandered around the Louvre had been with her aunt Izzy. 'How did you enjoy it?' she asked.

'Oh . . . incredible doesn't even begin to describe it,' Alice replied. 'And we didn't see the half of it.'

'You need a week to do the Louvre — properly, that is,' Shay commented.

'You're so right,' Alice replied. 'We're going back again tomorrow,' she said.

'Anyway, Charles thought we'd better call home in case you were wondering about us,' she went on.

'We assumed when we didn't hear from you that you were having a good time,' Shay said, recalling that Reeve had mentioned his father and Alice several times during the past week.

'We are. Believe me,' Alice repeated. 'But we left Stuart's Cove in such a hurry, we didn't give you the time of our return flight. We land in Vancouver on Saturday around six in the evening,' she went on to explain. 'Charles has arranged for us to spend the night with friends who live near the airport and then we'll catch the three-o'clock flight home to Stuart's Cove on Sunday afternoon.'

Shay quickly jotted down the times on the notepad near the phone. 'Fine. I'll pass that on to Reeve,' she said. 'Thanks for calling, Alice. Give Charles my best, and enjoy the rest of your holiday,' she added before hanging up.

'Was that Aunt Alice?' Mandy had

appeared at the back door just as Shay was writing on the notepad.

'Yes,' Shay said. 'She called to say she and Dr. Walker are having a great time and that they'll be back on Sunday.'

'You mean tomorrow?' Mandy asked, surprise in her voice.

'No, darling, next Sunday. They're staying one more week,' Shay said.

'That means Emma is staying for only one more week,' Mandy commented woefully. 'I sure wish Emma and her dad didn't have to leave.' She sighed heavily. 'And I wish Reeve — '

'Sweetheart, I know how much you've been enjoying having Emma around,' Shay quickly cut in, not sure she wanted to hear what Mandy had been about to wish for, though she had a good idea. 'But Emma and her father live in New York and when their holiday here is over, they'll be going back,' she stated, ignoring the stab of pain her words elicited.

Mandy's expression was decidedly glum, telling Shay all too clearly how deep her daughter's attachment had become to Emma. The girls had developed the kind of closeness and the type of friendship that would, if nurtured, last a lifetime. But even more troubling was the case of hero worship Mandy had developed for the man who was her father.

During the past two weeks, Shay had watched Mandy's eyes light up each afternoon when Reeve returned from the clinic. To her surprise and to his credit, Reeve had treated Mandy with the same fatherly affection he showed Emma, giving her equal attention, never excluding her or making her feel like an outsider.

The fact that Reeve behaved as if Mandy was his daughter only served to intensify Shay's feelings of guilt, but even more distressing was that Mandy appeared to have forsaken her mother's company in favor of Reeve's.

Hurt by what she saw as her daughter's defection, Shay had debated about cutting the amount of time

Mandy spent with Reeve and had contemplated refusing to allow Mandy to accompany him and her half sister on their nightly outings. But in the end, Shay hadn't had the heart to deprive Mandy of the attention her father bestowed on her, an action that would undoubtedly have resulted in tears from Mandy and questions from Reeve, questions she wasn't prepared to answer.

'Can't they stay longer?' Mandy asked, cutting through Shay's wayward thoughts.

'I don't think so,' Shay replied, not wanting to give Mandy false hope. 'I know how much you've enjoyed having them here, Mandy, but Emma's dad has an important job to go back to, and their home is in New York.'

'I'm really going to miss them,' Mandy said, her voice laden with sadness.

'Me, too,' Shay said softly, surprising herself. Annoyed, she picked up her purse and keys from the counter.

'Come on, sweetheart. Emma's waiting, and we've got shopping to do.'

★　★　★

An hour later, Shay lifted the last bag of groceries into the back of the station wagon and closed the door.

'Mom. That's the clinic over there, isn't it?' Mandy asked, pointing to the one-story building halfway down the block on the opposite side of the street.

'That's right,' Shay confirmed, moving to unlock the car doors.

'Can we go and see if Emma's dad is still there?' Mandy asked. At her words, Emma, who had been standing next to her half sister, gazed eagerly up at Shay.

Words of refusal instantly leaped to Shay's lips, but with two pairs of cornflower blue eyes staring hopefully at her, she could only nod in assent.

After crossing at the traffic light, they approached the clinic and Shay silently sent up a prayer that they had missed Reeve, that he'd already left. Her prayer, however, went unanswered as the door of the clinic opened and Reeve emerged into the bright sunshine.

'Hello there! This is a nice surprise,' Reeve said, his smile encompassing everyone.

Shay felt her heart flip-flop in her breast in response to his smile. He looked tanned and healthy and devastatingly attractive, wearing an olive golf shirt and matching cotton slacks.

As Reeve bent to effortlessly scoop Emma into his arms, Shay noted that the lines of strain around his eyes and mouth when he'd arrived in Stuart's Cove two weeks ago were no longer in evidence.

'What brings you to town?' Reeve asked as he lowered Emma onto the sidewalk and reached out to playfully tug Mandy's ponytail.

'We were grocery shopping,' Mandy announced, grinning up at her father.

'I see,' came Reeve's reply. 'Have you had lunch yet?' The question was directed at all of them.

'No,' Mandy replied before Shay could respond.

'Good. Because I'd like to invite you three lovely ladies to join me for lunch,' Reeve said.

'Can we go to Roxy's?' Mandy asked, naming her favorite restaurant. 'They make really good hamburgers,' she told him. 'We've eaten there before, haven't we, Mom?' Mandy swiveled to gaze up at her mother.

'What do you think, Shay?' Reeve shifted his gaze to meet Shay's and frowned a little when he saw the hesitation in her eyes.

Ever since that unforgettable kiss they'd shared in the kitchen, he'd been aware of her determination to avoid being alone with him and, needing the space himself, he'd done his best to comply with her unspoken request. But he'd found it increasingly difficult to banish from his thoughts the memory of her response or the emotions she had aroused in him.

'Mom?' There was a hint of exasperation in Mandy's tone and Shay felt a blush creep across her cheeks when she realized they were waiting for her reply.

'Sorry . . . Roxy's is fine,' Shay said, managing, for the girls' benefit, to force a little enthusiasm into her voice.

'Yeah!' Mandy grinned at Emma. 'Roxy's is down the street and round the corner,' Mandy said. 'Come on, Emma, I'll race you.'

'Hold on a minute, girls.' Reeve's authoritative tone brought both daughters to a halt. 'This is a public sidewalk, don't forget,' he cautioned. 'Instead of running, why don't the two of you walk and play follow the leader, that way you can keep an eye out for other pedestrians?' he suggested, softening his directive with a winning smile.

His words were met with silence and, seeing the familiar stubborn glint in her daughter's eyes, Shay held her breath in anticipation of a protest.

'Okay,' Mandy responded after a brief hesitation, before turning to Emma. 'I'll be the leader, 'cause I know the way,' she announced.

234

Emma nodded eagerly in response, and seconds later Mandy began to walk on ahead, with Emma close behind.

Mandy's quick compliance only served to confirm Shay's fears about Mandy's shifting affections. Annoyance rippled through Shay, knowing that had she disciplined Mandy, her daughter would most definitely have argued before reluctantly doing as she was told.

'Is anything wrong?' Reeve asked, noting Shay's tight-lipped expression.

'What could possibly be wrong?' she countered, unable to eliminate the displeasure from her voice.

'Shay? What is it?' Reeve insisted, putting his hand on her arm to prevent her from following the children.

★ ★ ★

A shiver of awareness chased up Shay's arm at the contact. 'Nothing,' she said, trying to ignore the way her pulse was skipping crazily beneath his fingers. 'I'm a little on edge, I guess. It's been a busy week,' she added, unable to meet his gaze, knowing her excuse sounded feeble. 'We'd better catch up with the girls,' she said and, breaking free, began to move away.

To Shay's relief, Reeve didn't pursue the matter. As they fell into step, she realized with a start that the emotion raging through her was jealousy. She was jealous of Reeve, jealous that he had won over Mandy with his warmth and easygoing charm, jealous that their daughter appeared to have accepted him without reservation.

★   ★   ★

'Hmm . . . decisions, decisions,' Reeve said as he glanced up from the menu he'd been perusing. 'Have you decided what you're going to have?' He let his gaze slide over Shay's bent head, noting the tension in her shoulders, wondering anew what she'd been upset about as they'd walked to the restaurant.

'I have,' Mandy declared.

'What about you, Emma?' Reeve asked and smiled when his daughter simply nodded. 'Shay?' He glanced across the table at her, thinking she looked decidedly attractive in her coral T-shirt and matching pedal pushers. Her skin was delicately tanned, giving her heart-shaped face a healthy glow, and he liked the way her hair curled softly just below her chin. Gone was the wild coltish look he remembered so well and in its place a new femininity, a maturity and quiet confidence that stirred his senses.

'I don't know,' Shay replied, continuing to browse through the menu, aware all the while of Reeve's eyes on her. She felt her pulse pick up speed and fought to ignore the fluttery sensations in the pit of her stomach.

She drew a steadying breath, telling herself that the ache gnawing at her insides had everything to do with her craving for food and nothing whatsoever to do with a different kind of hunger, a hunger only Reeve could arouse or appease.

'Here comes the waitress,' Mandy announced as a young girl arrived at the table carrying a pitcher of ice water.

'Hello, folks,' the waitress greeted them before filling each of the four water glasses on the table. 'Are you ready to order? Or would you like a few more minutes to decide?'

'I'm ready,' Mandy piped up. 'I'd like a cheeseburger with fries, please.'

The waitress set the water jug on an empty table nearby and quickly wrote the order. 'And you, miss?' she asked, turning to Emma.

Reeve said, 'She'll have — '

'I'd like a cheeseburger and fries, too, please,' Emma announced, much to her father's and Shay's astonishment.

'Thank you,' said the waitress as she turned to Shay. 'Ma'am?'

'Ah . . . I'll have the same,' Shay replied, recovering quickly, noting the anxious expression on Emma's face as she watched and waited for her father's reaction.

Shay instantly threw Reeve a warning glance, praying he wouldn't draw attention to Emma this time, that he'd act as if nothing unusual had happened and simply give the waitress his order.

Reeve caught the flicker of warning in Shay's eyes and to give himself some extra seconds cleared his throat and carefully closed the menu. 'You'd better make that four cheeseburgers and four fries,' Reeve said, managing to keep his tone even, while his heart thundered inside his chest like a herd of wild horses riding across the plains. 'Ah . . . does anyone want a milk shake?'

'I do!' Mandy jumped in. 'A strawberry one, please.'

With a casualness he was far from feeling, Reeve turned to his daughter. 'Emma?' He hoped he wasn't pushing too hard, but the need to hear her speak again was almost overwhelming.

'Yes, please, Daddy,' Emma replied. 'But can I have a chocolate one?' she asked.

I'd give you the moon if I could,

Reeve wanted to shout. He checked the impulse while his heart leaped into his throat as he struggled to maintain an outwardly calm composure. 'Chocolate it is,' he said, relief and joy cascading over him. 'Shay?' He met her gaze across the table.

'Chocolate for me, too, please,' Shay said, her eyes eloquently giving him both approval and encouragement.

He turned to the waitress. 'Two strawberry and two chocolate shakes,' Reeve said, handing the young girl his menu, wondering momentarily if it was all a dream.

'Thank you. I'll be right back with those milk shakes.' Pocketing her order pad, the waitress hurried away.

'Oh, Reeve, I forgot to tell you that Alice called just before we left,' Shay commented, keeping his attention away from Emma.

'Really? How are the honeymooners? Are they having a good time?' he asked, glad to follow Shay's lead, fighting the temptation to bombard Emma with questions to confirm that she'd indeed left her silent world behind.

He'd been stunned when she'd given the waitress her order and felt sure that had he not caught the warning Shay had thrown his way, he could well have spoiled the moment by overreacting.

For reasons he would probably never know or fully understand, Emma had been testing him. But in view of her quick response to his question a moment ago, Reeve was reasonably confident he'd passed the test with flying colors.

'They're having a wonderful time,' he heard Shay reply and had to drag his thoughts back to the conversation. 'But then, Paris is the perfect place for a honeymoon,' Shay went on.

'What's a honeymoon?' Mandy suddenly asked.

Reeve watched in fascination as Shay's cheeks turned a bright shade of pink.

'Well . . . ah,' Shay began.

'A honeymoon,' Reeve began, coming

to her rescue, 'is the holiday a couple take after they get married,' he explained.

'What do they do on a honeymoon?' Mandy asked, obviously finding the topic of interest and enjoying her father's attention into the bargain.

'Well, most couples simply like to spend time together,' he said.

'But what do they do?' Mandy persisted.

Reeve hesitated, not sure whether to be charmed or annoyed at Mandy's tenacity. 'That depends on where the couple go for their honeymoon,' he replied. 'Alice and my father went to Paris, and there are lots of things to see and do in Paris, like visiting the museums or climbing up the Eiffel Tower,' Reeve went on.

'I've been to the Eiffel Tower,' Mandy said proudly. 'But that wasn't much fun,' she told him. 'If I was going on a honeymoon, I'd go to Disneyland.'

'Me, too,' Emma piped up.

It was all Reeve could do to smother

the laughter bubbling up inside him. The urge to reach out and lift Emma out of her chair and into his arms was strong, but he controlled it.

Glancing at Shay, he caught the look of amusement dancing in the depths of her blue eyes and suddenly an emotion he couldn't quite define gently squeezed his heart, robbing him momentarily of breath.

The waitress chose that moment to return with their milk shakes, effectively distracting him. Beside him, the sound of a childish giggle brought his attention back to Emma as he watched her lean over to whisper into Mandy's ear, he quietly marveled once again at the miracle that had taken place.

He had his daughter back. The relief spearing through him was like nothing he'd ever known before. Shay had been right when she'd predicted that Emma would simply start talking. And as he lifted his gaze to the woman sitting opposite, he was struck with the realization that Shay's presence and her cool and unshakable confidence had gone a long way to ease his troubled mind.

Throughout the past two weeks, he'd been enjoying his days at the clinic and the evenings spent with Shay and the children, enjoying, too, a growing contentment as well as a level of peace he hadn't experienced in a long time.

Silently, Reeve acknowledged that not even in those early and happier days of his marriage to Louise could he ever recall feeling this depth of harmony or contentment. His marriage had begun to unravel long before the baby was born, but Emma's arrival had forced them to try harder, at least for a while.

In the end, Louise's unreasonable behavior, her overprotectiveness toward Emma, and her unwillingness to let Reeve play the role of father, had eventually eroded what remained of his feelings for his wife. But he'd often wondered if Louise simply hadn't been capable of being happy, not with him, not with anyone.

'Daddy, you're not drinking your milk shake.' Emma's voice cut through Reeve's musings and for the second time in less than half an hour, his heart expanded with love and gratitude that her days of silence appeared to be at an end.

'You're right,' he said, leaning forward to pick up the glass from the table and take a sip. 'Ah, here come the cheeseburgers,' he added when he saw the young waitress approach.

Throughout the meal, Emma laughed and talked, making up for those weeks when she hadn't spoken at all. Reeve watched his daughter with a mixture of love and pride, thinking all the while that he would never forget this day.

'We'd better be getting back,' Shay announced once they'd finished eating.

Reeve took care of the check, and as Shay followed the girls out into the sunshine, she couldn't recall a meal she'd enjoyed more, smiling to herself as she listened to Emma's nonstop chatter.

'Can I ride back with you in your car, Daddy?' Emma asked when Reeve joined them on the sidewalk.

'Sure,' Reeve replied, surprised and pleased by her request.

'Can Mandy come, too?' Emma wanted to know.

'Of course,' Reeve responded readily. 'As long as it's all right with her mother,' he added, throwing Shay a questioning glance.

'Please, Mom? Can I?' Mandy pleaded.

Shay bit back the sigh hovering on her lips. She knew she was being foolish, but she couldn't seem to come to terms with Mandy's defection. Somehow, she summoned a smile. 'Sure,' she said.

Grinning at each other like coconspirators, the girls ran ahead.

'I thought I'd stop by the lumberyard and pick up a couple of pieces of plywood for the tree-house roof,' Reeve said as they began to retrace their steps to the clinic.

Shay's irritation of a moment ago dissipated at his words, touched that he seemed determined to fulfil the promise he'd made to Mandy. 'You really don't have to, you know,' she said.

'I can't go back on my promise,' Reeve replied. 'Besides, it's the least I can do and my way of saying thanks.'

'For what?' Shay asked, casting him a sideways glance.

'For what Mandy's done for Emma . . . what you've both done,' he amended. 'You had more faith in my daughter's recovery than I did, and I'm sure just being around the two of you has helped give Emma back her self-confidence.'

A warmth stole over Shay at his words. 'You played a part, too,' Shay assured him. 'You were patient with her, and you stopped pressuring her. Emma's lucky to have a father like you,' Shay said, her tone sincere, ignoring the tiny voice inside her head telling her Mandy deserved a father, too.

Reeve stopped Shay in midstride, his hand grasping her arms as he turned her to face him. 'Thanks. It means a great deal to hear you say that,' he added a hint of huskiness in his voice.

Shay's heart began to trip a little faster and beneath his fingers she felt her skin quiver as a familiar need began to spread through her.

'Reeve Walker! I thought it was you.' The unfamiliar voice cut through the tense silence.

Reeve turned to face the newcomer. 'Jake McGraw! As I live and breathe,' Reeve said, breaking into a wide smile.

Shay watched as the two men enthusiastically shook hands.

'It's good to see you, buddy,' Jake said.

'Likewise, I'm sure,' Reeve replied. 'Jake, you remember Shay O'Brien.'

'Of course,' came the reply. 'Shay. It's nice to see you again. How's the bed and breakfast doing? I hear you've reopened your aunt's place.'

'Hello, Jake,' Shay responded. 'Yes, the inn is open and so far I've had a few visitors. Which reminds me. I'd better be getting back . . . '

'Are you coming to the fishing derby tomorrow?' Jake asked.

'Fishing derby?' Reeve repeated.

'Stuart's Cove's annual fishing derby,' Jake spouted. 'I'm the organizer this year,' he explained. 'The derby itself starts at dawn and closes at five. There are lots of prizes to be won and they're announced during the potluck dinner and dance at the south end of the promenade.'

'Sounds like fun,' Reeve said. 'What do you think, Shay? The girls would enjoy that, wouldn't they?'

'Yes, I suppose,' Shay replied haltingly.

Reeve turned back to Jake. 'Would you happen to know if my father still keeps his boat down at the marina?' he asked.

'Yes, he does,' Jake said. 'I can count you in, then?'

'Absolutely,' Reeve replied. 'But probably not at dawn,' he amended.

'No problem, you can start anytime,'

Jake said. 'I've got to run. I'll see you folks tomorrow. Maybe we'll get a chance to catch up on old times,' he added before hurrying off down the street.

Reeve grinned at Shay as they fell into step once more. 'I'll have to make a trip up to the house later and hope I can remember where Dad keeps the keys to his boat. It's been a long time since I did any fishing,' he added, nostalgia creeping into his voice now.

'Fishing? Are we going fishing?' Mandy asked as they reached the girls waiting outside the clinic.

'Not today,' Reeve said.

'When?' both girls asked at the same time.

'How would you like to take part in a fishing derby tomorrow afternoon?' Reeve asked.

'What's a derby?' Emma asked.

'We don't have a boat,' Mandy noted seconds later.

'We do have a boat,' Reeve assured Mandy. 'And a fishing derby is a contest to see who can catch the biggest fish,' he explained to Emma.

'Neato!' Mandy said. 'But won't we need a fishing pole? Mom, do you have a fishing pole?'

'There might be a few in the garden shed, but I don't know what kind of condition they're in,' she said. Aunt Izzy had liked to fish and had stored her equipment in the shed.

'My father keeps all his fishing gear on the boat,' Reeve said. 'At any rate, we can figure out these details later,' he suggested. 'Come on, you two, my car's around the side of the building.' He ushered the children ahead of him. 'We'll see you back at the inn.' With a fleeting smile for Shay, he followed the girls.

Shay was surprised at the feeling of loneliness that settled over her as she drove back to the inn. Ever since the doctor in that small hospital in the French countryside had handed Shay the tiny miracle that was her daughter, she had vowed to love and protect

Mandy and put her child's needs before her own.

For the past nine years, Shay had done her best to keep that promise and with Aunt Izzy's help, love and support, she had succeeded. She'd had to make a few sacrifices along the way, occasionally juggling her own life and career in order to make sure she was always there whenever Mandy needed her.

With Aunt Izzy gone, Mandy was the only family Shay had left in the world and since returning to Stuart's Cove, Shay had had to accept that from now on there would be just the two of them. Besides, they didn't need anyone. They had each other.

Reeve and Emma's intrusion in their lives had changed everything. Never having had a positive male influence in her life before, Mandy's growing admiration and obvious fascination with Reeve was understandable. Hadn't she herself been equally as fascinated ten years ago?

Shay bit down on the inner softness

of her mouth, annoyed with the route her thoughts had suddenly taken. Ten years ago, she'd been a naïve, lovesick fool and she'd paid the price for her foolishness. But somehow, watching her daughter fall under Reeve's spell was more than she could take.

All at once, those feelings of jealousy she'd had earlier toward Reeve returned, but beneath the jealousy lay another emotion, one Shay wasn't sure she was ready to face. And that emotion was fear. Fear that if Mandy learned the truth about Reeve, she would never forgive her mother for the deception and for depriving her of the right to know the identity of the man who was her father.

9

When Shay brought the station wagon to a halt at the rear of the inn, she immediately noticed the blond-haired young man, wearing shorts and a T-shirt, sitting in a patch of shade and leaning against a large backpack.

'Hello!' Shay greeted him as she opened the driver's-side door and stepped out.

'G'Day,' said the young man, his tanned youthful features breaking into a welcoming smile. 'I wondered if you had a room available?' he asked in an accent that was unmistakably Australian.

'Yes, I do,' Shay responded. 'I hope you haven't been waiting long,' she went on as she moved to the rear of the wagon.

'Not very,' came the reply. 'Need a hand?'

Shay flashed a grateful smile. 'Thanks. I've got a few bags of groceries to carry in,' she told him.

'Glad to help,' said the newcomer as he joined her at the rear of the car.

'How long are you planning on staying?' Shay asked as they walked together toward the back door.

'I'm not sure,' he answered. 'One night, maybe two. Is it a problem?'

'Not at all. Stay as long as you like,' Shay assured him. Unlocking the door, she moved inside, relieved to note that the kitten hadn't been up to any tricks while she'd been gone. 'There on the counter is ideal,' she told him as she set the grocery bag she was carrying onto the kitchen table. 'I'm Shay O'Brien, by the way,' she added, offering her hand.

'Jonathan Stevens,' he responded with a firm handshake.

'How long have you been touring, Jonathan?' Shay asked as he followed her out into the sunshine once more.

'Please call me Jon. Ah ... I left

home the first week of July,' he responded.

'And where's home?'

'Brisbane, Australia,' he told her, confirming her earlier impression.

'You're a long way from home. How long are you planning on being away?' she asked, handing him another bag of groceries.

'Until I've seen the world, or until my money runs out, whichever comes first,' he added with a cheeky grin.

Shay laughed. 'If you're counting your pennies, the campsite on the other side of town might be more in line with your budget,' Shay told him after she'd quoted the nightly rates she charged.

'I passed the campsite on the way in. It's full to overflowing,' Jon said. 'The ranger said this is a busy weekend, what with the fishing derby tomorrow,' he explained.

'Ah . . . right. I'll tell you what,' Shay said, making a snap decision. 'I'd be happy to throw in dinner for that price,' she said, feeling sorry for him.

'Really? That would be super! You have a deal! Ta very much,' Jon said.

'Bring in your backpack, and I'll show you to your room,' Shay said once she'd finished putting away the groceries.

'Would it be all right if I took a shower?' Jon asked when he returned with his backpack.

'Of course,' Shay replied. 'I'll show you where everything is,' she added as she led the way upstairs.

Half an hour later, looking decidedly more presentable in a clean white T-shirt and beige shorts, Jon returned to the kitchen where Shay was preparing chicken cordon bleu in readiness for their evening meal.

'Is there anything I can help you with?' Jon asked.

'Thanks, but everything's under control,' Shay said. 'There's some lemonade in the fridge, help yourself to a glass,' she invited as she put the last piece of chicken into a baking dish ready for the oven. 'Tell me, Jon. Where has your trip taken you so far?'

It was while Jon was regaling Shay with a story of his first few days on the road that Reeve and the girls returned.

Even before he reached the door to the kitchen, Reeve heard Shay laughing. His heart kicked against his ribs at the sound. He'd forgotten how melodious, how provocative her laugh was and his mouth curved into a smile.

But the moment he opened the door, the smile froze on his lips at the sight of the tall and tanned, handsome young man standing next to Shay, practically breathing down her neck.

Shay was smiling at the man with a warmth and openness that sent Reeve's blood pressure soaring. Suddenly, a dark and dangerous emotion, one he immediately recognized as jealousy, twisted like a knife inside him.

'I hope I'm not interrupting anything,' Reeve said, his tone icy, his anger barely in check.

'Oh, hello Reeve! I didn't hear your car,' Shay said, turning to greet him.

'Where are the girls?' she asked, her glance sliding past him.

'They went down to the tree house to play,' he replied stiffly, his gaze intent on the handsome young man beside her. 'I don't believe I've had the pleasure,' Reeve said, disapproval evident in his tone and in his whole demeanor.

Reeve saw the flicker of apprehension in the young man's eyes but felt neither regret, nor remorse.

'Ah . . . no,' Jon began, his voice wavering slightly.

'Reeve, this is Jonathan, Jonathan . . . ' Shay glanced at Jon once more, smiling apologetically for having forgotten his surname.

'Stevens, Jonathan Stevens,' the visitor obliged, extending his hand, though a trifle tentatively. 'Your wife has been very kind . . . '

Reeve heard Shay's sharp intake of breath and noted the flush that darkened her cheeks in response to the youth's words. 'No! No, we're not

259

married,' Shay denied hotly. 'Jon, this is Reeve . . . Dr. Walker. He and his daughter Emma have been staying here,' she explained.

'Oh, I see,' Jon said, although it was quite clear by the puzzled expression on his face, he didn't see at all.

'Jon is from Australia,' Shay said, bewildered by the tension simmering in the air. Reeve's arrival had caught her off guard, but she was at a loss to understand what had prompted his show of hostility toward Jonathan.

'Really,' Reeve said, unimpressed.

'Ah . . . Shay,' Jon said. 'I think I might just take a stroll down to the beach. What time should I be back?' he asked, already edging toward the door.

'Dinner's at six,' Shay told him with a smile.

'Fine. I'll see you around six, then,' he said, reaching for the door handle.

'I thought you only served breakfast,' Reeve commented once Jon had departed.

'That's right,' Shay said, puzzled by the dark expression on Reeve's face.

'But I thought maybe the price of a room is more than Jonathan's budget can handle. I told him I'd include dinner,' she said, annoyed that she should feel the need to explain anything to Reeve.

'If you want to stay in business, you'll have to harden your heart to all the hard-luck stories you're bound to hear,' Reeve said.

Anger sizzled through Shay and she lifted her head to meet his gaze. 'One, Jon didn't give me a hard-luck story, as you put it. And two, how I run the inn is none of your business and I'll thank you to keep your opinions to yourself,' she added. Her tone was sharper than she intended, she knew, but his comment had been patronizing, to say the least.

They stared at each other for several long seconds as tension arced between them. All at once, Reeve's features relaxed into a dazzling smile, sending Shay's heart into a tailspin.

'You're absolutely right,' he said

solemnly. 'Please accept my apologies.'

But before Shay could gather her scattered thoughts, the door burst open and the children came running inside.

'Daddy, you said you were coming down to the tree house,' Emma said coming to a halt beside her father. 'Mandy and me waited and waited.'

'I'm sorry, pumpkin,' Reeve said, aware that this apology sounded much more sincere than the one he'd just given Shay. 'I came in to put shorts on, but I got a bit distracted,' he added, all the while thinking that 'distracted' didn't begin to describe what he'd felt when he'd walked in and found Shay laughing with Jonathan Stevens. 'If you wait right here, I'll run upstairs and change and be back in two shakes of a dog's tail,' Reeve went on.

This comment brought a giggle from both children. 'A dog's tail!' Mandy repeated. 'You aren't a dog and you don't have a tail,' she told him.

Reeve grinned. 'How about two shakes of a cat's tail, Patches's tail,' he teased. 'I'll be right down,' he added and quickly withdrew.

Shay poured the girls a glass of lemonade each as they waited for Reeve.

'I didn't think to buy a hammer and nails when I was at the lumberyard,' Reeve said when he returned. 'I know your aunt always kept tools. Would you mind if I poked around in the shed to see what I can find?'

'Of course not,' Shay replied.

'Will the roof be on the tree house by tonight?' Mandy asked hopefully as she and Emma followed Reeve from the kitchen.

'I don't think so,' Reeve said. 'Come on, let's see what we can find in the shed, shall we?'

Left on her own, Shay busied herself preparing the remainder of the meal. As she chopped the apples and walnuts for a Waldorf salad, her thoughts drifted back to those tense moments before Reeve had offered his apology. She was still at a loss to understand his aversion to Jon and hoped that the atmosphere at dinner wouldn't be too strained.

* * *

To Shay's relief, Reeve was coolly polite to Jon throughout the meal, but she noticed that each time she spoke to Jon or asked him a question, he would throw Reeve a nervous glance before giving her an answer.

The children instantly took a shine to the handsome young Australian, intrigued by his accent, taking it in turn to ask him endless questions about his country and his family.

'Jillian and Jenny are fourteen and sixteen. Typical teenagers who drive my mom and dad crazy,' Jon said in response to Mandy's question regarding the ages of his two younger sisters. 'Jillian is blond like me, but Jenny's hair is much darker. They don't look like sisters at all.' He paused and let his gaze switch from Mandy to Emma and back again. 'You and Emma look more like sisters than they do,' he commented with a laugh. 'How old are you, Emma?' Jon went on, unaware of the small but deadly bombshell he'd just dropped.

Shay felt her heart ricochet against her ribs in sudden panic and frantically she tried to think of a way to divert attention from what she knew was a potentially dangerous conversation.

'I'm six,' Emma told him proudly. 'I'll be seven in November,' she added.

'And how old are you?' Jon asked, turning to Mandy.

'I'm — '

'Would anyone like dessert?' Shay blurted out in a desperate attempt to prevent the approaching catastrophe.

'Mom! It's not nice to interrupt!' Mandy scolded. 'I'm nine years old,' she told Jon. 'And my birthday is March fourteenth.'

For Shay, the silence that followed Mandy's words was deafening. All she could hear was the sound of her heart drumming a thunderous tattoo against her breast. She threw Reeve a frightened glance, silently praying he wasn't paying attention. Her prayer wasn't answered.

'Nine . . . ?' Reeve repeated, almost to himself, his gaze on Mandy, and Shay felt her heart shudder to a halt when a frown creased his handsome features.

'What's for dessert, Mom?' The question came from Mandy, and Shay had to force a smile as she turned to her daughter.

'Ah . . . there's fresh fruit salad and ice cream,' Shay said, surprised that her voice sounded normal. 'Jon? Can I interest you in dessert?' she asked. Pushing back her chair, she stood up and with trembling fingers began to gather the dishes. 'Mandy, pass me your plate, darling. You, too, Emma.' Shay knew she was babbling but she couldn't seem to stop. The urge to look at Reeve was overpowering, but she checked it, fearful he would see the guilt as well as the truth in her eyes.

'You're nine?' Reeve said again, his eyes on Mandy, and Shay's heart plummeted like a skydiver free-falling from a plane.

'That's right,' Mandy quickly confirmed, flashing her father a smile.

Continuing to stare at Mandy, Jon's remark concerning the likeness of the girls leaped into Reeve's mind and he was suddenly struck by Mandy's strong resemblance to Emma, a resemblance he'd noticed but thought merely coincidental. On closer examination, the comparison was rather startling. Mandy had the exact color of hair and eyes as Emma.

Sisters . . . they could be sisters. Reeve's brain tested the theory as he performed some quick mental arithmetic. The result was mind-boggling.

Was it possible? Could Mandy be his daughter? The idea that it might be true shook him to the core.

Glancing at Shay, he thought he glimpsed a flash of guilt in her eyes before she looked away. She seemed agitated, and he noted she had deliberately avoided his gaze. Feelings of anger and frustration welled up inside him and tempted as he was to haul her out of the kitchen and into a secluded corner to confront her, the presence of the children and the Australian Adonis sitting across the table, prevented such a dramatic move.

Besides, maybe he was wrong. Maybe he was simply jumping to conclusions. After all, on the night they'd made love, Shay had told him she was protected, that she was on the Pill. But he recalled treating a number of women who'd become pregnant while on the Pill.

If he was right — his breath caught in his throat and pain squeezed at his heart — it would explain Shay's rather defensive reaction whenever he'd tried to question her about Mandy's father.

'Daddy? Don't you want any dessert?' Emma's question cut through Reeve's wayward thoughts.

With an effort, he controlled his riotous emotions. 'Dessert? You mean there's actually some left? You two haven't eaten it all?' he teased, hoping Emma wouldn't notice his preoccupation. There was little he could do at the moment to confirm his growing suspicions. He would have to wait until the children were in bed before he could talk to Shay. But talk to her he would.

'We haven't eaten it all,' Emma replied, smiling at her father. Reeve grinned back, thinking all the while that if Mandy was his daughter, he doubted Emma would have a problem accepting that piece of astonishing news.

'Mom, Reeve wants fruit salad, too,' Mandy said.

'Coming right up,' Shay replied. Keeping her attention on the task, she spooned fruit into a bowl and set it in front of him.

'May I have a scoop of ice cream?' Reeve asked politely, determined to try to force Shay to make eye contact with him, needing to see a reaction, hoping to garner something, however slight, from the expression in her eyes.

He held his breath and watched as she scooped ice cream onto the fruit, but just as she lifted her head to hand him the bowl, the telephone rang and immediately she swung her gaze away from his.

Reaching toward the counter, Shay picked up the receiver. 'O'Brien's Bed and Breakfast Inn. How may I help you?' Shay asked brightly. She was silent for a moment, as she listened to the caller. 'Yes, of course, he's right here,' she said. 'Reeve, it's Jake McGraw. He wants to talk to you.'

Setting the receiver carefully on the counter, she turned and proceeded to put the lid on the ice-cream carton before crossing to the fridge.

For the last five minutes, she'd been aware of his eyes boring into her, almost as if he was willing her to meet his gaze. His reaction to Mandy's announcement of her age had told Shay quite clearly the path Reeve's thoughts had taken, and she sensed it was only a matter of time before he confronted her and asked the question she'd been dreading since the moment he'd appeared at his father's wedding.

She could lie, of course, but she doubted Reeve would accept a denial, doubted he would believe her without an interrogation.

'No problem, Jake,' Reeve said. 'I'll pop over and take a look at her right now. I'll see you in about ten minutes.'

'Where are you going, Daddy?' Emma asked the moment her father replaced the receiver.

'I have to pay a visit to a patient,' Reeve replied. 'I shouldn't be more than an hour,' he added.

'If it's an emergency, shouldn't the call have gone through your pager?' Shay asked.

'Normally it would have, but Jake didn't call the clinic,' Reeve said. 'He called my father's place first, thinking I was staying there. When he didn't get an answer, he decided to try here,' he explained.

'Will we still be able to go for a walk

on the beach when you come back?' Emma wanted to know.

Reeve glanced at the clock. It was already seven. 'I doubt it, pumpkin, but we'll see,' he added, noting the disappointment that clouded his daughter's eyes.

'If you girls want to help me with the dishes, we can go for a walk on the beach when we're done,' Shay suggested.

'And I'll keep you company. If I may,' Jon piped up.

'Okay!' Emma and Mandy were quick to agree.

Shay noted the look of annoyance that came and went in Reeve's eyes. 'Fine,' he said tightly. 'I've got to go. But I'll be back in time to read you a bedtime story,' he told Emma as he dropped a kiss on her forehead.

'Bye, Daddy,' Emma said, showing no signs of concern at his departure.

The children and Jon helped Shay clear the dinner table and wash the dishes and twenty minutes later found them all walking along the sand. A cool breeze off the water tugged gently at Shay's hair as she watched the girls race toward the Twin Rocks.

If Jon noticed Shay's preoccupation as they drew near the rocks, he made no comment. And when the girls ran up to challenge him to a race along the sand, he happily obliged, leaving Shay to wander to the edge of the Twin Rocks on her own.

She climbed several feet to a flat spot and sat down to gaze out across the water, watching the sun's rays as they danced on the waves. Red and pink colors streaked across the sky like a painter's brush strokes, giving the appearance here and there of flames shooting up from below the horizon.

The moon hung high, waiting impatiently for the sun to make its exit and reminding Shay of another moonlit night, a night she'd never forgotten, a night engraved on her heart and in her memory forever.

Her graduation dance, a special night

in any young girl's life, but for Shay an evening that had been no more memorable than any other, until Reeve arrived. Bored and restless, she'd been leaning against one of the pillars in the gymnasium when some sixth sense had alerted her to his presence.

She'd watched with bated breath as he'd scanned the dancers on the floor and she'd known in that moment he was searching for her. When he'd started to walk toward her, she'd felt her heart gather speed to thunder inside her breast, practically drowning out the music coming from the band onstage.

When he'd stopped in front of her and asked her to dance, she'd almost fainted on the spot, scarcely able to believe that her dream, the one she'd been having every night since her birthday, was actually coming true.

With a sigh of contentment, she'd stepped into his arms, to the place she'd yearned to be for so long. She'd floated around the room on a cloud of pure happiness, aware of nothing and no one but the man holding her. Tiny sparks of sensation had rippled through her, leaving a trail of longings in their wake, restless longings that left her breathless and dazed.

The music stopped and she'd almost groaned aloud in protest when Reeve pulled away. Feeling strangely bereft and desperate to prolong their encounter, she'd asked him if he'd give her a ride home, and when he'd told her he was walking, she hadn't thought twice about inviting herself along.

They'd taken the shortcut over the Twin Rocks and before long she'd had to remove her high-heeled shoes and panty hose in order to gain better traction on the rocks' slippery surface. When they reached the tiny sandy cove where the two rocks joined, Reeve had been the one who suggested they take a breather and like a hero from another era, he'd gallantly placed his jacket on the sand for her to sit on.

That's when he'd started talking about New York, about becoming a doctor, about getting away from Stuart's Cove and with each word he uttered, she'd felt all her own hopes and dreams were being snatched out of her hands one by one.

Numbed by the pain washing over her as she'd listened to his plans, plans that hadn't included her, plans that would take him away from her, she'd asked Reeve if he'd kiss her goodbye, simply wanting one sweet memory to hold on to, one small dream to come true.

And it had, beyond her wildest imaginings. The moment Reeve's mouth touched hers, the world began to spin out of control. Like the tornado that lifted Dorothy to the magical Land of Oz, she and Reeve were suddenly thrown into the chaotic center of a twister that transported them higher and higher to a new and different dimension, the place where only true lovers go, only true lovers know.

For an agonizing moment, concern for her and the possible consequences of their actions somehow had given Reeve the strength to hold back the raging storm of passion threatening to overwhelm them. But Shay had quickly assured him that she was protected, that there would be no consequences. At the time, she'd believed she was telling the truth.

In the storm's quiet aftermath, as she'd lain in the warmth and shelter of his arms, she'd gazed up at the moon and stars wondering, after such a shattering experience, how they could still be in the sky. She'd drifted off to sleep and been awakened with a kiss from Reeve, a kiss that had resulted in a second magical journey, one as equally memorable and unforgettable as the first.

Too much in awe of what had happened between them, Shay hadn't been able to think of a single thing to say as they walked back to the inn in the early hours of the morning. After a whispered promise to call her later, Reeve had dropped a brief and

277

decidedly unsatisfying kiss on her lips, before gently but firmly urging her inside.

Shay had tiptoed to her room, falling into bed to replay over and over in her mind those earth-shattering moments when their souls had joined. She'd grown restless with need as she'd dreamily recalled the way Reeve's body had felt beneath her questing fingers, how his taut muscles had rippled in response to her touch, how magnificent his love-making had been.

As she drifted off to sleep, she'd ached to hold him once more, to know again the dizzying heights of the passion only he could arouse. To her surprise, she'd slept for most of the day and Aunt Izzy hadn't disturbed her, no doubt letting her recover from the graduation dance.

By late afternoon, when she hadn't heard from Reeve, she'd grown increasingly anxious and more than a little concerned. But confident he would keep his promise, she'd curbed the impulse to seek him out, feeling more than a trifle shy at the thought of seeing him again.

After dinner, when Aunt Izzy realized she'd forgotten to pick up her medication from the drugstore, Shay had volunteered to drive into town in the hope that she might run into Reeve.

She'd cruised the streets looking for him to no avail. Puzzled and a little desperate, she'd made a detour on the way home and had driven to the Walker house, but there had been no sign of activity from within, nor had there been any cars parked in the driveway.

On her return to the inn, she'd held her breath hoping her aunt would tell her Reeve had called while she'd been out, but no such message had been forthcoming. Much later, when she'd crawled into bed, Shay hadn't been able to stop the flow of tears that slowly soaked her pillow.

Without as much as a goodbye, Reeve had left Stuart's Cove. He'd gone to pursue his dreams, his future in

New York, and in leaving he'd dashed all Shay's adolescent hopes and dreams.

Less than two weeks later, when her period failed to appear, she'd had a fleeting moment of panic, then just as quickly dismissed the absurd thought. But when another week passed, a week spent fighting the overwhelming nausea that greeted her each and every morning, Shay had known she was pregnant.

She'd paid a visit to the hospital in Fernhaven to confirm her suspicions and had asked the doctor how she'd become pregnant while taking the Pill, prescribed a month before as a means of regulating her often irregular and overly heavy menstruations.

Unperturbed by her question, the doctor had pointed out a number of reasons for the pregnancy, perhaps she hadn't taken the medication long enough or the medication had not been prescribed in a strong enough dosage.

Regardless of whichever reason applied in her case, nothing changed the hard fact that she was carrying Reeve's child.

'Mom! Mom! We're going back now. Are you coming?' Mandy's voice cut through Shay's musings, bringing her back to the present.

'Yes, I'm coming,' she replied. Rising, she hopped onto the sand beside her daughter, noting as she did that several large dark clouds had rolled in, hiding both the moon and the sun and making it appear as if someone had suddenly dimmed the lights.

'What were you doing, Mom? I yelled at you twice,' Mandy said as she slid her hand into Shay's, sending a warmth chasing through her.

'Sorry, darling, I was daydreaming,' Shay said, smiling down at her daughter.

'What about?' Mandy asked.

'Oh . . . just about another summer as warm and lazy as this one,' she replied.

Emma and Jon waited until she and Mandy caught up and together they made their way back to the inn. The girls were soon bathed and ready for bed and it was while they were seated at the kitchen table enjoying a bedtime snack of milk and cookies that Reeve returned.

This time, Shay knew the moment Reeve's car pulled into the driveway. When the back door opened, Emma let out a squeal of delight before hopping down from her seat to run to her father.

With a pang, Shay noted the look of longing that flashed in Mandy's eyes as she watched Reeve lift Emma into his arms.

Patches chose that moment to jump into Mandy's lap, offering a much-needed distraction.

'Have you fed her?' Shay asked, glad to have a reason herself to avoid Reeve's gaze.

'No, I forgot,' Mandy said, sliding out of her chair and heading to the pantry.

'Well, I think I'll say good-night,' Jon said, rising from his chair. 'I want to write a couple of letters before I go to bed and mail them before I leave tomorrow,' he explained with a quick glance at Reeve.

'Aren't you going to stick around for the fishing derby tomorrow?' Reeve asked as he lowered Emma into the chair she'd vacated a few minutes before.

'No, I don't think so,' Jon answered. 'Surfing's more my sport. Good night, kids,' he added before making his retreat.

'Good night!' the girls chorused.

''Night, Jon,' Shay said before she began to clear the glasses from the table.

'Are you going to read me a bedtime story now, Daddy?' Emma asked.

'Of course,' came Reeve's prompt reply. 'Ah . . . Mandy. Would you like to listen, too?' he asked.

At his words, Mandy turned and, obviously thrilled at being included, smiled winningly at her father. 'Yes, please,' she replied.

'Great,' Reeve said. 'All you two have to do is decide which story you want me to read.'

'I didn't bring too many books with

me,' Emma said. 'But Mandy has lots in her room.'

'Why don't we let Mandy pick the story?' Reeve suggested and received another dazzling smile from the child he'd already begun to believe was his.

Shay was relieved a few minutes later when Reeve, Emma and Mandy disappeared down the hall into Mandy's room. For the next half hour, she busied herself tidying the kitchen, polishing the toaster, wiping the sink until everything on the counter sparkled like a shiny new coin.

She'd been tempted several times to escape to her room, but recalling the brief but intense glance Reeve had thrown her way before he'd followed the children, she'd known that running would be foolish, and hiding nothing more than an exercise in futility.

Not even a closed bedroom door would stop him, of that she was sure. One way or another, Reeve intended to confront her and find out the truth about Mandy's parentage . . . tonight.

10

'Is it true?' Reeve's deep voice vibrated across the room, and Shay gasped in surprise at the sound of it.

For the past five minutes, she'd been standing at the bay window in the living room gazing out at the ocean, her nerves stretched to breaking point, waiting for Reeve to appear.

Taking a deep steadying breath, she turned to face him, noting instantly the tension in his body, the tautness of his facial features, as well as the pulse throbbing at his jaw.

'Is what true?' she asked, astonished that her voice came out sounding calm and collected, emotions she was far from feeling.

'Don't play games with me, Shay,' Reeve warned. 'You know damn well what I'm asking. Just tell me the truth. Is Mandy my daughter?' He held her gaze, and his breath, and waited.

'Yes, Mandy is your daughter,' Shay said in a voice that was firm and clear and deceptively strong. She watched as he swayed momentarily at her words, almost as if he'd been buffeted by a gale-force wind.

'I knew it!' His words hissed into a room that was humming with tension and rife with emotion. 'My God! Shay! Why didn't you tell me? I had a right to know.'

Shay hugged herself, trying with difficulty to ward off the old pain and heartache threatening to resurface. 'You're right. You did,' Shay acknowledged quietly. 'But first I have a question for you, Reeve. Why did you sneak off to New York like a thief in the night without even saying goodbye?'

Reeve cursed under his breath and ran an agitated hand through his hair. 'Damn it, Shay. I didn't sneak off to New York,' he dismissed angrily. 'You knew I was leaving. I'd told you I was leaving.'

At his words, Shay felt her own anger slowly push its way to the forefront. 'You promised you would call, Reeve. I thought a promise from you was worth something. It seems I was wrong.'

'I did call, damn it!' Reeve retorted, taking the wind out of her sails.

'You did?' Her question was a breathless whisper as she met his gaze.

'Yes, I did,' he reiterated.

'Aunt Izzy didn't tell me . . . she didn't say — '

'She probably didn't know it was me,' Reeve cut in, and Shay caught the flash of guilt and the glimmer of regret that appeared briefly in his eyes. 'I didn't leave a message.'

'Why not?' Shay asked, still trying to come to terms with the fact that he had called.

'Because I didn't know what to say, to her . . . or for that matter, to you,' came Reeve's reply, a sharp but distinct ring of truth in every syllable. 'What the hell could I say?'

Shay swallowed the lump of emotion

287

lodged in her throat. Reeve's silence, the fact that he hadn't bothered to call had been the hardest to bear. 'You could have said something . . . anything — ' She broke off abruptly, suddenly fighting back tears. 'We made love that night, Reeve, or have you forgotten?'

'I haven't forgotten,' Reeve replied. 'I've never forgotten,' he mumbled almost inaudibly. 'You told me you were protected, that you were on the Pill. Did you lie to me, Shay? Why didn't you contact me when you found out you were pregnant?'

'I did call you,' Shay said, and this time it was Reeve's turn to be surprised. 'I got your telephone number from your father,' she told him. But it had taken her almost the entire weekend to pluck up the courage to dial the number Charles had given her. 'When I got through, a young woman answered,' Shay went on, managing to keep her tone even. 'I asked to speak to you, and she

288

laughed and said something about you being the man she was going to marry.'

'Louise . . . ' The name came out in an exasperated breath. 'Jason's sister. Jason was my friend all through med school. He's the one who invited me to stay with him in New York. Louise just liked to play tricks. She did stuff like that all the time,' Reeve explained. 'She was joking.'

'Really? So it's just a coincidence that you happened to marry a woman named Louise?' Shay countered, her tone mocking.

'No, they were one and the same person,' Reeve told her as a rush of color came and went on his face. 'But I wasn't dating her then. That first year in New York, I barely knew which end was up, what with studying and all the hours I spent at the hospital. I rarely saw Jason, never mind Louise, and I certainly didn't have time for any extracurricular activities, much less a relationship — ' He broke off.

'But you did marry her,' Shay persisted, refusing to let him off the hook.

Reeve met her gaze, his gray eyes unblinking. 'Yes, I did marry her,' he confirmed, though there was a bleakness in his voice and in the depth of his eyes. 'Wait a minute . . . Why didn't you leave a message?'

Shay was silent for a moment. Though Reeve might not have been aware of it at the time, Louise had set her sights on him from the start. Shay recalled with clarity the underlying warning she'd heard in the other woman's voice, and because Reeve had left Stuart's Cove without a word, without bothering to see her or talk to her, Shay had had no choice but to assume the woman was speaking the truth, and that what they'd shared that night on the beach meant nothing to him.

'What difference would it have made?' Shay challenged. 'Your career was all that was important to you then.'

And still is, she refrained from adding. 'You just told me you didn't have time for anything other than your studies and your work at the hospital. Telling you I was pregnant wouldn't have changed anything.'

'Of course it would,' Reeve said tightly. 'What do you take me for, Shay? I would have supported you and the baby, at least financially,' he told her. 'How did it happen?'

Amusement trickled through Shay at the absurdity of the question, but somehow it helped to defuse the tension still simmering inside her. 'I would have thought, being a doctor and all, that you would know exactly how it happened,' she said dryly, and saw his mouth twitch with the beginnings of a smile.

'Very funny,' Reeve responded. 'You said you were on the Pill. If you weren't lying, there has to be another reason, a medical one. Am I right?' he asked.

Shay relented. 'Yes. It had been prescribed to me. But I was told I hadn't been taking the prescription long enough to ensure protection, either that or the dosage wasn't strong enough,' she explained. 'But that's all water under the bridge,' she hurried on. 'What's important now is what's best for Mandy.'

'On that, at least, we agree,' Reeve replied.

'Then I hope you'll also agree with me when I say that it's in Mandy's best interests to leave things as they are,' Shay said. Selfish as it might appear, Shay had reached the conclusion that to tell Mandy the truth and have her father leave shortly thereafter would be entirely too traumatic for the child, at least to Shay's way of thinking. 'Mandy is a happy, contented, well-adjusted child, and I don't see any reason to disrupt or change that.'

Reeve stared at her in stunned surprise. 'You have to be joking.' His voice was edged with ice. 'I'm her father. Do you think I'm just going to walk away from that? Besides, Mandy has a right to know the truth, just as I had a right to know.'

'But you already have a daughter,' Shay argued. 'You have Emma, and I have Mandy. Can't you just leave things the way they are?' While the notion was both simplistic and perhaps more than a little selfish, Shay could see no other solution to the dilemma they faced.

The pulse at Reeve's jaw began to throb once more. 'I disagree. You'd have to be blind not to have noticed that during the past two weeks Mandy has become attached to me and I to her. She needs a father. She needs me,' he amended. 'And I don't think she'd be too upset to learn the truth, that I am her father.'

'You can't tell her,' Shay insisted, trying to keep the panic from her voice. 'At least not yet,' she added, backing off from the look of anger that leaped into his eyes, unwilling to admit that he was right about Mandy's growing attachment to him, or about the fact that she needed her father.

'And pray tell, when would be a good time?' Reeve asked sarcastically. 'I have commitments. I can't stay here indefinitely until you decide it's the right time. Emma and I have to get back to New York.'

At his words, a pain tore through Shay but she refused to acknowledge it. Bravely she held her ground. 'That's my point exactly,' she countered. 'What good would it do to tell Mandy the truth now? In another week you'll be gone.'

'Damn it, Shay! There has to be a solution, a compromise . . . something.' Reeve sighed in frustration.

'Fine. When you think of it, let me know,' Shay said, and without waiting for a reply she hurried from the room, leaving Reeve staring after her.

In the silence that followed Shay's departure, Reeve sank onto a nearby armchair and dropped his head onto his hands. Raking his fingers through his hair, he let his mind drift over their heated exchange.

Silently, he acknowledged that there had been faults on both sides with miscommunication or lack of communication playing a large part. He wasn't at all proud of the way he'd behaved ten years ago. Shay hadn't deserved to be treated as a one-night stand, but that's exactly what he'd done.

But what happened between them that night had shaken him to the core, and he realized that he'd been unwilling to deal with the depth of emotion she'd aroused in him, fearful she would somehow derail the future he'd carefully mapped out for himself.

He'd been selfish, too caught up in where his life and his career were going to allow anything or anyone to distract him from the goals he'd set. He'd treated her badly and, coupled with Louise's insensitive response, he couldn't really blame Shay for not telling him about her pregnancy.

But an indisputable fact still remained. Mandy was his daughter. She was his flesh and blood. A sense of wonder he'd never thought he'd feel again washed over him like a balm to his soul.

The first time he'd experienced this same euphoria was when his friend and colleague at Manhattan Metro told him of Emma's successful delivery by cesarean section, almost seven years ago.

After assuring himself that Louise was fine, he'd gone immediately to the hospital nursery. He still remembered vividly those heart-stopping moments when he'd set eyes on Emma for the very first time.

At a mere six pounds, she'd looked so small, so helpless yet so incredibly beautiful. He'd stood in awe, staring down at his daughter, scarcely able to believe she was actually his. He'd gently stroked her pink cheek, and when Emma's tiny fist had thrust out toward him and her hand had curled tightly around his finger, he thought his heart would explode as feelings of love and wonder and pride swamped him, bringing tears of joy to his eyes.

He wasn't sure how long he'd stood there, entranced by the tiny baby before him, but a nurse had had to shake him to get his attention. He'd been about to protest that he wasn't ready to leave, when she'd asked if he wanted to hold his newborn daughter.

When the nurse placed Emma in his arms, Reeve thought he must look like Goliath. Gazing down at the precious bundle, he'd felt awkward and inept as well as totally captivated.

Recalling those wonderful moments, Reeve felt a twinge of sadness at the fact that he hadn't been there when Mandy was born. But during the past two weeks, she'd nudged her way into his heart to find her own place there. Her straightforward manner and ready acceptance of Emma's silence had charmed and impressed him, and he acknowledged that Shay deserved a great deal of credit for raising such a bright, loving and caring child on her own.

Finding out Mandy was his daughter

was quite simply icing on the cake. Now he had two remarkable and wonderful daughters. He was twice blessed. But Shay had been right when she said that telling Mandy the truth wouldn't be fair, not when his and Emma's return to New York was only a week away.

With a sigh, Reeve rose from the chair and slowly made his way upstairs. While he still had no solution to his dilemma, there was one thing he was absolutely sure of. He wasn't walking away from his responsibilities this time. There had to be an answer. He just had to find it.

★　★　★

It was almost noon on Sunday, and the girls were already waiting in Reeve's car, eager to head into town to take part in the fishing derby. Most of the morning had been spent in preparation for the outing.

Reeve had driven to his father's

house in search of the keys to the boat moored at the dock and had returned triumphant. Shay, with Emma and Mandy's help, had made a casserole of lasagna, and Shay had retrieved several fruit pies from the freezer as part of her contribution to the potluck supper.

Shay and the girls had said their farewells to Jon, who'd headed out after breakfast with a promise to return.

'You won't have to worry about missing any potential customers today,' Reeve told Shay as he pulled the car out of the driveway. 'Everyone's sure to be at the fishing derby.'

'I left a note on the front door saying we'd be back around nine tonight, just in case,' Shay told him.

Reeve laughed, the deep rich sound sending a shiver of longing through Shay. 'There's nothing like telling a potential burglar the place will be empty all afternoon,' he said, shaking his head, but there was a teasing quality to his tone.

In the sky above them, a few white

fluffy clouds floated lazily by, none looking in the least like a threat to the hot and sunny weather the area had been enjoying the past two weeks.

Through the open window of the car, the breeze off the water tugged gently at Shay's hair, trying to free the strands she'd woven into a short braid earlier that morning. She was wearing shorts and a matching top in swirling shades of purple, blue and pink and had added a dash of lipstick as an afterthought.

Behind the wheel, Reeve in a pair of navy shorts and a navy and white golf shirt, looked relaxed and carefree, his expression giving away nothing. He'd made no mention of their discussion the previous evening, not that she'd expected him to in front of the children, but Shay had spent a restless night wondering just what he would decide to do regarding hers and Mandy's future.

Beneath lowered lashes, Shay glanced at Reeve, taking in his handsome profile, the strong jawline, the passionate mouth, his aquiline nose and eyes the color of shimmering diamonds. Her heart skipped a beat as she continued to study him, and suddenly her fingers itched to run through his hair, to feel again its silky texture, to urge him closer and taste again the need, the passion, only he could arouse.

A moan of longing almost made it past her lips. Dear heaven! What was happening to her? She shifted restlessly in her seat.

Throughout the drive into town, Emma and Mandy chattered excitedly about the fish they hoped to catch, and a short time later, as Reeve pulled the car into one of the few remaining parking spaces at the rear of the marina, Shay was surprised at the crowd already gathered to watch or participate in the event.

After dropping off the food they'd brought at the food tent, they made their way down the boat ramp. Reeve quickly located the twenty-five-foot

301

cabin cruiser that belonged to his father, and once on board he helped his daughters put on life jackets before hopping ashore to register for the fishing derby and purchase a bucket of live bait.

On his return, Reeve fired up the engine, and as he eased the boat away from its berth, they followed a number of boats of various sizes making their way out into open water. Before leaving the inn, Shay had made certain the girls applied sunscreen and had insisted that while on the water, they wear baseball caps to protect them from the sun's harsh rays.

'Where are we going, Daddy?' Emma asked as her father opened the throttle, steering the boat away from the rest of the fleet.

Reeve flashed Emma a smile. 'When I was your age,' he began before turning his attention to the water ahead, 'my father — your grandfather — would take me fishing almost every weekend, and one of his favorite spots was just off the end of the cove,' he said.

'Is that where we're going?' Mandy asked.

'That's right,' Reeve replied.

On reaching their destination, a spot half a mile off the headland, Reeve dropped anchor and soon, with their father's help, Emma and Mandy baited a hook and tossed a line over each side into the water.

Shay relaxed on deck, enjoying the gentle sway of the boat as it rocked and rolled over the waves, and watched with growing admiration the way Reeve divided his time between the girls, first chatting with and encouraging one, then turning to the other, giving each child individual attention.

A number of boats had also dropped anchor around them, while others trolled back and forth. Now and then a shout would ring out over the water as a salmon was reeled in by someone on one of the nearby boats.

'I've got something!' The squeal of excitement that accompanied Mandy's words brought Shay to her feet. 'I've got something!' Mandy repeated.

Reeve quickly moved to her side. Keeping his voice low, he gently coaxed and instructed Mandy, who eagerly followed his instructions and in no time reeled in and netted her catch. 'Well done! It's a beauty,' he said, giving Mandy a pat on the back.

Clearly thrilled beyond measure at having caught her first fish, Mandy threw herself at her father, hugging him tightly. 'Thank you! Thank you! I couldn't have done it without you. That was the best.'

Watching the embrace, Shay had seen the glint of tears that appeared in Reeve's eyes before he blinked them away, and suddenly an emotion she refused to acknowledge, an emotion she thought she'd safely locked away gently squeezed her heart.

'Daddy! Daddy!' Emma's urgent shout, less than ten minutes later, startled everyone, and only Reeve's lightning reflexes prevented Emma from losing the rod.

This time, however, Reeve had to reel in Emma's catch, but Emma didn't seem to mind, grinning happily at Mandy. The girls compared catches, with Emma's being declared the winner. But when Reeve asked if they wanted to try again, both declined and soon the two girls disappeared below deck.

Shay followed the girls and, after pouring lemonade and setting out granola bars for them to snack on, ventured up on deck once more to find Reeve occupying one of the seats, a fishing rod held loosely in his hand.

'Want to give it a try?' Reeve asked.

His question startled Shay as he'd given no indication that he knew she was watching him. 'Ah . . . no, that's all right,' she said, realizing with a frown that she'd left her straw hat in the cabin below.

Reeve twisted in the seat and the smile he sent her way would have melted an iceberg. 'Tell me, when was the last time you did something just for the pure enjoyment of it?' he asked lazily.

Shay hesitated, the need for her hat forgotten as her heart flip-flopped inside her breast in response to his smile.

It was the opening Reeve needed. 'Too long, I bet,' he quickly asserted. 'Come on, Shay, take it,' he urged and, rising from the seat, held out the fishing rod, its line dangling over the edge and disappearing into the water.

Unable to resist the tug of his attraction or the offer, Shay took the rod, and when Reeve shifted over, she sat down in the seat he'd just vacated.

'Ah . . . this is the life,' Reeve commented with a contented sigh. Stretching his legs out in front of him, he cupped his hands behind his head. 'Knowing how to relax has become a lost art. There's just too much stress in the world today,' he said. 'I'd forgotten how soothing it is to simply take time out for yourself, to get off the treadmill, at least for a little while.'

Shay said nothing, content to listen to the low murmurings of his voice, wrapped up in the simple joy of being with Reeve, knowing it wouldn't last, knowing she would treasure this memory for a long time to come.

'Mind you, I must admit it's much easier to relax around here,' Reeve continued. 'There's something about Stuart's Cove that's synonymous with peace and quiet. It feels good to leave the pressures of work behind. That's something I've never been very good at,' he confessed. 'I think I've spent half my life hurrying toward the next goal instead of enjoying the journey.' His gaze drifted toward the horizon.

'Most people make the same mistake,' Shay said. 'It's human nature . . . Oh! My goodness!' Shay shot to her feet as the rod she'd been holding suddenly jerked in her hand. Tightening her grip, she pulled back on the rod, watching it bend under the strain.

'Hey! I'd say you've got something there.' Reeve jumped to his feet. 'Pull.

That's it. Now reel her in a little,' he instructed, his voice calm and encouraging. 'Easy. That's the way,' he praised.

Shay did as Reeve directed and quickly reeled in a few feet of line before pulling back again on the rod and reeling in again. All at once, she felt as if her arms were being wrenched out of their sockets as her underwater adversary suddenly took off in an obvious attempt to catch her unawares and break free.

'Oh . . . I can't hold on!' Shay said, struggling to keep her balance as the line spun out. Her palms were already slick with perspiration as she began to reel in the line again, and her shoulders ached from both the effort and the strain of holding on so tightly.

'Here, I'd better give you a hand,' Reeve said, moving to stand behind her. Putting his arms around her, he added his hands to the rod and Shay immediately felt the strain on her arms, on her entire body, diminish.

'We've got it! We've got it.' Reeve's

voice so close to her ear brought a smile to her lips and for a few seconds Shay allowed herself the luxury of leaning back, savoring his strength, delighting in the feel of his hard muscular body pressed against hers.

Suddenly, without warning, the line snapped, sending them both stumbling backward. Reeve recovered first and bracing his feet on the deck, managed to prevent them from falling.

'Too bad. That's the one that got away,' Reeve said, a hint of frustration in his voice. 'You had a surefire winner there.'

Somewhat in a daze, Shay stared up at the broken line blowing harmlessly in the breeze. Reeve, his arm still around her, made no move to release her as the scent of lemons, lilacs and lace assailed his senses and a familiar heat began to spread through him, leaving a trail of need in its wake.

'You can let go now,' Reeve said softly, telling himself he should move away, break the contact. But he couldn't seem to get his body to obey.

Slightly unnerved by what had happened and by the warm caress of Reeve's breath tickling her ear, Shay released her grip on the rod and slowly turned to face him.

As her body brushed his, Reeve drew a ragged breath as desire streaked through him like a bolt of lightning. Shay lifted her gaze to meet his and when he found himself staring into eyes as deep and fathomless as the ocean, he lost what little self-control he had left.

Tossing the fishing pole onto the deck, he swooped down to capture Shay's mouth in a kiss that had every nerve aching with need, every cell screaming for more. She was bewitched, she had to be. No other woman had ever been able to drive him to the edge with just a single solitary kiss. He couldn't seem to get enough of her, the taste of her, the scent of her, the feel of her. It was almost as if she'd cast a spell on him, branded him hers exclusively, totally, completely.

Shay's world was spiraling out of control as Reeve's mouth worked its magic, sparking a response she was only too willing to give. Her body melted against his like candle wax touched by flame, and the resulting fire raging through her swept everything in its path, leaving a trail of desire that had her trembling with need and aching for his possession.

Suddenly, the boat began to sway dramatically as the wake from several crafts speeding by created a large swell that knocked them off-balance and sent Reeve sprawling onto the seat, while Shay stumbled in the opposite direction.

'Mom! What was that? What happened?' Mandy's voice held more than a hint of fear. Both girls had appeared at the top of the steps leading down to the small cabin.

'It was just some fools going too fast and passing too close,' Reeve told them, annoyance edging his tone as he sat up. 'Shay, are you all right?' he asked, glancing to where Shay had come to rest against the wheel.

'I'm fine,' she lied, avoiding his eyes, turning instead to the children, noting the look of fear on their faces. 'That was a bit scary, wasn't it?' she acknowledged and both girls nodded. 'But we're all right,' she added, giving them a reassuring smile. 'Have you finished your snack?' she asked. Finding her sea legs once more, she joined the girls.

'The lemonade spilled,' Emma said, her bottom lip trembling a little.

'We were just trying to pour some more when the boat started to rock,' Mandy explained.

'Not to worry,' Shay said. 'Why don't you two help your fath — ' Shay blundered to a halt and threw Reeve a panicked glance. She swallowed before continuing, 'Ah . . . help Reeve gather up all the things that fell out of the tackle box,' she amended. 'I'll clean up the lemonade before everything gets sticky.'

The girls quickly moved to do as she'd suggested, and Shay escaped to the relative sanctuary of the cabin. Tearing several strips of paper towel from the roll she'd brought with her, she began to wipe up the spill, unable to believe that she'd almost blurted out the truth.

She blamed Reeve's kiss for muddling her senses and numbing her brain. A kiss she could have avoided, a kiss she could have prevented.

Liar! You couldn't have prevented it because you wanted him to kiss you, a little voice inside her head taunted. Shay wiped vigorously at the spill, knowing the voice was right, that stopping Reeve and denying herself the sweet torture of his kiss had been the furthest thought from her mind.

She'd welcomed the kiss, reveled in it, and on the fact that Reeve had been as equally aroused. She could no more have resisted the chance to feel his mouth on hers, to taste again the sweet torment of need only he could arouse, than walk across the water.

Shay sat back on her haunches, the spill forgotten. Fool that she was, she'd remained faithful to Reeve these past ten years.

It always had been Reeve . . . always would be Reeve. And that could only mean one thing. She still loved him, always had loved him, would never stop loving him.

The realization hit her like a blow to the solar plexus and with a broken sob she began to rock back and forth, one hand hugging her stomach while the other covered her mouth to prevent any sound from escaping.

Fool! Fool! her heart cried out in despair. Ten years ago she'd fallen in love with a man more interested in his career than in sustaining a relationship. But while she acknowledged that Reeve cared deeply for Emma and for Mandy, too, his career was still an important factor in his life and she doubted that would change.

And while he might want to make

room for Mandy in his life, his new position as head of the Trauma Unit at Manhattan Metro would undoubtedly take up a great deal of his time. That, together with the difficulty of maintaining a long-distance relationship with his daughter, would make it impossible for Reeve to give Mandy the kind of fatherly attention she needed and deserved.

Shay could only hope that Reeve would see things her way and agree not to reveal the truth to Mandy. Yes, she was being selfish. And yes, she was asking a great deal. But there really wasn't any other choice. Was there?

11

Fearful the children might come looking for her and find her weeping, Shay drew a steadying breath, brushing away the tears tracing a path down her cheeks. She felt emotionally drained and wished she could magically whisk herself back to the inn and avoid spending the remainder of the afternoon and evening with Reeve.

Silently she admonished herself for being a coward, and after mopping up the last of the lemonade from the floor, she grabbed her straw hat and headed up on deck. Wrapped up in her own misery, she hadn't noticed that the boat was moving. Glancing at Reeve manning the wheel, his eyes on the water watching for potential hazards, she thought he looked as handsome as a sea captain in a romantic novel.

The children were seated at the stern,

and Mandy appeared to be pointing out different landmarks to Emma.

'Where are we heading?' Shay asked, blankly staring at the water ahead, maintaining a polite distance.

'Nowhere in particular,' Reeve replied. 'I thought we'd had enough fishing for one day.'

'Hmm,' Shay mumbled her agreement.

'I told the girls we'd take a ride across the cove and back again, then head for the marina,' Reeve continued, keeping his eyes on the water.

'Fine,' Shay said before retreating to sit with the girls.

As the boat sped across the water, the wind wrestled with Shay's braid, tugging it free to whip her hair about her face. The children laughed with glee. Shay joined in, but if her laughter sounded hollow, she was the only one who noticed.

Half an hour later, Reeve deftly maneuvered his father's cruiser back into its berth. Shay collected the hamper from the cabin and helped the children remove their life jackets before climbing ashore.

'Why don't you and the girls take the salmon up and get them weighed in and measured?' Reeve suggested. 'I'll clean up here and meet you up on the promenade in, say, twenty minutes.'

'Okay,' Shay replied, unwilling to argue. They'd hardly spoken since the kiss they'd shared, and throughout the jaunt across the cove Shay had been glad of the children's chatter, which had helped to fill the silence.

The girls each carried their respective catches to the weigh-in table. Ten minutes later, leaving the salmon packed in ice for collection later, they climbed the ramp leading to the promenade.

'Can we have ice cream?' Mandy asked.

'*May* we,' Shay automatically corrected. 'And yes, you may,' she added with a smile for both girls.

'What flavor are you going to have?'

Emma asked Mandy as they stood in line at the ice-cream store's counter.

'I don't know. What are you going to have?' Mandy asked.

In the end the girls both chose bubblegum-flavored ice cream, while Shay picked chocolate chip. While they ate their ice-cream cones, they strolled along the promenade. The atmosphere was indeed festive and the bright mood of the people milling around began to rub off on Shay, lifting her spirits.

In the heat of the afternoon sunshine, the ice cream began to melt and, finding a vacant seat along the promenade, Shay and the girls sat down to finish their cones. With the help of a few small napkins, Shay tried to keep the mess to a minimum.

'There you are,' Reeve said as he came up behind them.

'Oh . . . hello!' Shay responded.

'I was beginning to wonder if I was going to find you in this crowd. There's quite a turnout today,' he commented as he came around the seat.

'Daddy, do you want some of my ice cream?' Emma asked, thrusting sticky hands and dripping cone at her father.

Reeve recoiled a little and tried to keep a straight face when he saw the messy state both Emma and Mandy were in. Ice cream was streaked on their cheeks and around their mouths was a layer of bubblegum lipstick. 'Ah . . . no, thanks,' he replied as he watched Shay dabbing ineffectively at the mess, using one of the smallest napkins he'd ever seen.

'Don't move. I'll be right back,' Reeve said and true to his word returned a few moments later with a handful of large napkins. 'Allow me,' he said and smiled as Shay relinquished her post with a heartfelt sigh of relief.

'I think we've had enough, don't you?' Reeve said as he tossed what little remained of Emma's and Mandy's cones into a nearby trash can and proceeded to wipe the children's hands and faces. Having had the foresight to dampen several of the napkins in a water fountain, order was soon restored.

'Can we go look in the toy-store window?' Emma asked, pointing to the store a little farther along the prom-enade, the minute her father had finished drying her hands.

'Okay,' Reeve replied. 'We'll be right behind you,' he said as the girls hopped down from the seat and scurried off.

Reeve turned to Shay and his smile widened when he saw the smear of chocolate at the corner of her mouth. His first impulse was to take her in his arms and kiss the smudge away, but he quickly curbed it when an emotion he couldn't define flashed in the depths of her blue eyes.

'You've got a smudge,' Reeve said and reached a hand toward her.

It was all Shay could do not to take a step back. Her eyelids fluttered closed and she held her breath trying to ignore the ripple of awareness chasing through her at Reeve's gentle touch.

'There,' Reeve said, but there was a slight catch in his voice.

'Thank you.' Shay opened her eyes, hoping he wouldn't notice that she'd begun to tremble.

'We'd better catch up with the girls,' Reeve said.

'I'll wait here,' Shay said, needing a few moments alone, finding his presence infinitely disturbing, especially now that she realized the depth of her feelings for him.

Reeve hesitated, then nodded.

He found the girls staring at a display of stuffed animals in the store's window.

'Daddy, Mandy thinks that one looks like Patches,' Emma said, indicating the orange, black and white fluffy toy near the front of the group of animals.

'Yes, I suppose it does,' Reeve agreed with a smile as he crouched to the children's level.

'And I think this one looks like Smoky,' Emma said, directing her father's attention to a larger toy.

'Smoky?' Reeve repeated. 'Oh, you mean Uncle Jason and Aunt Lisa's dog?

You're right, it does.'

'What kind of dog is he? I forget,' Emma said.

'He's a Shetland collie, and he's got the same coloring as Patches,' Reeve added.

'I wish I could have a dog,' Emma said with a wistful sigh.

'Sweetheart, we live in an apartment on the eighteenth floor,' Reeve said. 'It really isn't suitable for a dog. Dogs need a house with a nice big yard.'

'Couldn't we live in a house with a yard?' Emma asked.

'Houses with backyards aren't easy to find in the middle of New York City,' he teased gently.

'I didn't mean New York, Daddy. I mean right here,' Emma said.

'Here? You want to live here?' Reeve repeated, surprise echoing through his tone.

'Yeah. There are lots of houses with big yards here,' Emma said. 'I like it here. I like it a lot. And if we lived here, we could get a puppy and Mandy could come over every day and play with me and the puppy. And Mandy says we would go to the same school and we would always be best friends.' Emma came to a halt and watched her father's face, obviously wanting to see his reaction.

Stunned by his daughter's words, Reeve glanced from Emma to Mandy and saw an identical expression of yearning in the depths of both sets of blue eyes. 'I see you two have this all figured out,' Reeve said, not at all sure what to think, astonished that the girls had obviously talked to each other on the subject.

Encouraged no doubt by the fact that her father hadn't instantly dismissed the notion, Emma continued. 'Couldn't we please stay?' she asked, a plaintive note creeping into her voice. 'Mandy says she wishes she had a daddy just like you, and I told her I don't mind sharing, 'cause when I lived with Mommy, I didn't see you very much and I missed you and so I know what it's like not to have a daddy.' Out of breath, Emma came to a halt once more.

This time, the knot of emotion lodged in Reeve's chest made it impossible for him to speak. All that had registered of Emma's chatter had been the comment that Mandy wished she had a daddy just like him.

With a brief look at Mandy, who'd been silent throughout Emma's discourse, Reeve noted the blush on his eldest daughter's cheeks and noticed too that she was attempting to hide her embarrassment by looking down and kicking at the sidewalk.

He didn't doubt for one moment that every word Emma had uttered was true and all at once he realized that they'd just handed him the solution he was looking for. 'Out of the mouths of babes,' Reeve murmured as a feeling of excitement suddenly clutched at him.

'Daddy? Can we stay?' Emma asked again, a puzzled frown on her face as she waited for her father to continue.

Reeve quickly composed his features, wondering just how to handle this delicate situation. 'Sweetheart, your happiness means a lot to me, and I can promise you that I'll think carefully about all that you've said.' His tone was serious and he watched as Emma's eyes widened.

'Really?' she said, obviously surprised at his response, a look of hope shining from her blue eyes.

'Really,' he assured her. 'As long as you understand that whatever decision I make, it will be a decision I believe is best for us.' He wasn't about to offer false hope, but she'd certainly given him food for thought and the idea rolling around in his head warranted further exploration and consideration. 'I don't know about you two, but I'm hungry. Let's head for the food tent, shall we?' he suggested and as if sensing that this wasn't the time to plead or push her father any further, Emma nodded.

When Reeve and the children returned,

Shay immediately sensed something had happened. There was a thoughtful expression in Reeve's eyes, and the girls kept glancing at him before turning and whispering together almost conspiratorially. But tempted as she was to ask questions, Shay remained silent.

Reaching the food tent, they joined the rest of the crowd who'd taken part in the derby lining up to fill their plates from the colorful and extensive array of dishes set out smorgasbord-style on three long tables.

Bowls of green salads, bean salads and pasta salads were displayed, as well as hot and cold chicken dishes and several large casseroles with both meat and vegetable entrées. Barbecued ribs and roasts of beef were also available, along with an assortment of potato dishes.

On a smaller table sat a variety of desserts ranging from pies and cakes to jelly and cookies. Coffee urns were also in evidence. As they slowly made their way down the line, a number of townfolk stopped to chat to Shay, many asking when Charles and Alice were returning.

Behind her, Reeve was greeted with friendly smiles and warm handshakes, and Shay couldn't help noticing that even though he'd only been in Stuart's Cove for two weeks, he appeared to already know more of the townsfolk than she did.

She quickly reasoned that his time spent at the clinic accounted for the warmth of his reception, but as they carried their plates outside the tent to one of the picnic tables, Shay wondered fleetingly if Reeve's return to Stuart's Cove had made as much of an impact on him as it had on the town.

From the bandstand nearby, a group of musicians began to play. Over the next hour, the music was interrupted at different times to allow Jake McGraw to announce the winners in a variety of categories. Numerous prizes, donated by local sponsors, were handed out amid cheers and applause from participants and their families and friends.

Neither Mandy nor Emma won a prize, but they didn't seem to mind, not when Reeve hauled both children onto their feet and danced with them. With one daughter hanging from each hand, he spun them around and soon had them giggling and begging for more.

A second group of musicians took over on the bandstand and the tempo suddenly changed to a rousing polka. Over the rim of her coffee cup, Shay watched Reeve take first one child then the other and polka around the space in front of the bandstand.

The sound of the children's laughter and the sight of their happy, glowing faces told a joyful story and for a few minutes at least, Shay allowed herself to dream. Tears stung her eyes but she blinked them away, knowing that even if her dreams couldn't come true, this was a day she wouldn't soon forget.

'It's your turn.' Reeve's deep resonant voice, sounding slightly out of breath, sliced into Shay's distracted thoughts and a tremor ran through her when she lifted her gaze to find him standing next to her.

'I'm sorry?' Shay set her near-empty coffee cup onto the table.

'I told the girls we'd show them what dancing is supposed to look like,' Reeve said. 'Come on. You can't let me down,' Reeve insisted, offering her his hand. 'They're both sitting on the bandstand watching,' he told her before she could ask.

Shay knew she should refuse, knew she was only torturing herself by agreeing to dance with him, but she couldn't quite squash the rush of longing that pulsed through her as he waited for her answer.

He offered his hand and, telling herself this was just another memory to hoard away in that secret corner of her heart, she reached out to grasp it. At the contact, a quiver of sensation spiraled up her spine and, managing to allay the warning flutters in her stomach, she rose from the table and let Reeve lead her onto the small dance area.

It was only then that Shay realized the band had changed tempo once more and the rich mellow sound of a soulful saxophone filled the evening air. A number of couples were already dancing to the seductive rhythm, and when Reeve gently tugged Shay into his arms, she let out a sigh of pure contentment and prayed silently that Reeve wouldn't hear the thunderous roar of her heartbeat.

Nothing had ever felt so right. Wrapped in the haven of Reeve's arms, she felt as if she were floating on air. At every point of contact from shoulder to thigh her skin tingled from the shock of dozens of tiny explosions, and when she felt his lips brush her hair, she closed her eyes and savored the delight, the sweetness of the moment.

Dreamily, she inhaled the evocative male scent of him, wondered not for the first time what there was about this man that seemed to call out to her, to touch her soul. Her heart shuddered in her breast when his arm tightened to draw her closer, an action that sent a bolt of heat racing through her.

Her mind blurred for just an instant as desire sent her senses veering madly off course. Her fingers itched to explore the muscles at the back of his neck and comb through the silky smoothness of his hair; her mouth longed to trace a path up the column of his throat and sear kisses along his jaw until she reached his mouth; and her heart ached for his kiss, for the pleasure, the taste, the passion only he could arouse.

She felt like an angel in his arms and as he breathed in the heady scent of the sea afloat with rose petals, it was all Reeve could do not to bury his face in the feathery softness of her hair and nibble on the delicate curve of her neck.

Their bodies moved in perfect harmony, and his heart stumbled drunkenly against his ribs as an ache steadily spread through him, igniting a need that sent his blood pressure soaring and played havoc with his control.

Out of the corner of his eye he glimpsed the children waving at him from the bandstand and it was enough to bring to a halt the wildly erotic thoughts dancing in his head. With some effort, he reined himself in, wondering not for the first time what there was about Shay that aroused in him such a deep and unquenchable passion.

Deliberately now, he turned his thoughts back to those moments in front of the toy store when Emma had unknowingly pointed him toward a solution. Throughout their meal, he'd given considerable thought to the comments she'd made and the more he explored the idea that had subsequently sprung to life, the more he knew it was the answer he'd been searching for.

Drawing a deep breath which filled his head with the potent and erotic scent that was hers alone, he eased away from Shay. Her eyes remained closed and as he studied her features he noted the pink flush on her cheeks as well as her shallow breathing.

'It's been a wonderful day,' Reeve said, his breath fanning her cheeks and making her eyelids flutter.

'Hmm,' Shay said, keeping her eyes closed, afraid to open them for fear Reeve would see her love for him shining in her eyes. The music would end all too soon and these precious minutes in his arms would have to last her a lifetime.

'And to top it all, the girls came up with a solution to our problem,' Reeve said.

Shay came to an abrupt halt and felt her heart leap into her throat. Her eyes flew open and she gazed up at Reeve, apprehension chasing through her. 'The girls?' she repeated. 'You didn't tell Mandy . . . ?'

'No, I didn't tell Mandy,' Reeve assured her, annoyed that she'd even voiced the question.

She frowned. 'Then I don't under-stand.'

'Let me explain,' Reeve said. As they were no longer dancing, he ushered her to the edge of the dancing area to the quietest spot he could find. 'The girls were looking in the toy-store window earlier,' he began. 'Emma said that Mandy wishes she had a father like me. That's what gave me the idea.'

Shay's heart thudded ominously in her breast and she twisted her fingers together as anxiety tied her throat muscles into knots. 'Wh . . . What . . . What idea?' Her voice came out in a throaty whisper, sure that whatever the 'idea,' she would undoubtedly be on the losing end.

'That we should get married,' Reeve said without the slightest trace of emotion in his voice. 'Emma and Mandy will have a mother and a father. We'll be a family, providing them with a stable environment to grow up in.

'In the circumstances, I believe it's

the best solution,' he hurried on. 'You must admit that we've all gotten along rather well these past two weeks and there's no reason to think that won't continue.'

'Wait just a minute,' Shay said with barely suppressed rage. As she'd listened to his dispassionate speech, her fear had quickly given way to anger and disbelief. There had been no mention of love. In fact, there had been a hollowness, a detachment in Reeve's tone, that tore at her heart. 'You can't be serious. You're suggesting we get married?'

Reeve bristled at the scorn in her voice. 'That's exactly what I'm suggesting,' he replied, his jaw clenching to control the anger coursing through him. 'And if you'd just stop and think for a minute, you'd see that it's the only viable solution — '

'Daddy!'

'Mom!'

The sound of the girls' voices cut through Reeve's words. He threw Shay a warning glance telling her all too clearly that their conversation was far from over, before he turned to smile at the children.

'Hey, kids. What's up?' he asked, sitting down.

'Emma couldn't see you and my mom dancing anymore,' Mandy said.

'So Mandy stood up and that's when she saw you standing over here,' Emma jumped in.

'Then we came to find you,' Mandy finished.

'We were just having a rest,' Shay said. 'It's been a long day. I think it's time we headed home.'

'Aw . . . do we have to?' Emma and Mandy chorused, their glances moving to look at their father in the hope that he would take their side.

'Yes, we have to,' Reeve said. 'But not before we have one last dance,' he added, flashing a teasing grin at the girls. Reeve got to his feet and instantly each child grasped an outstretched hand and began to haul him back to the dancing area.

'I'll collect the salmon and meet you at the car,' Shay said, suddenly needing to get away.

'Good idea.' Reeve tossed the words over his shoulder.

Shay turned and began to wind her way between the picnic tables, acknowledging a farewell smile here, a goodbye wave there. Inside she was a mass of contradicting emotions.

Anger and rage at Reeve's obvious assumption that she would simply fall into his plans — his 'solution,' as he'd termed it — simmered just beneath the surface ready to erupt again at the slightest provocation.

But while Reeve's suggestion that they get married for the sake of the children had stunned her, somewhere near the region of her heart hope and a deep longing warred with the anger, leaving her feeling confused.

Resolutely she told herself that she'd be a fool to agree, a fool to marry a man who didn't love her. Oh, he cared for her, that much she knew, they'd been friends for too long for it to be otherwise, but regardless of just how convenient a marriage between them would be, regardless of the fact that she was hopelessly, desperately in love with him and regardless of the flame of desire that burned between them whenever they touched, she knew in her heart that a marriage without mutual love would be nothing more than a disaster waiting to happen.

But what about Mandy? The voice inside her head asked the question she'd been trying to push to the back of her mind. Didn't Mandy deserve to know her father? Could she in good conscience deprive her daughter of the love and guidance Reeve was both willing and eager to give?

12

To Shay's relief, the children chattered continually throughout the journey back to the inn. Beside her, she could feel the tension in Reeve and knew he was anxious to continue their conversation.

But by the time they reached the inn, Shay's head was pounding, and she knew that the pain throbbing insistently behind her eyes had everything to do with the emotionally charged day.

After the girls helped unload the car, Mandy scooted off to her room to get ready for bed and Reeve accompanied Emma upstairs.

Alone in the kitchen, Shay poured a glass of water and taking a seat at the table she swallowed several aspirin, hoping the medication would work fast. Dropping her head onto her hands, she closed her eyes for a moment.

'Are you all right?' Reeve's voice startled Shay. Annoyed that he'd caught her unawares, she stood up.

'I have a bit of a headache,' she told him, making light of the pain hammering at her temples.

'Too much sun,' Reeve suggested, fighting the need to close the gap between them and pull her into his arms. He could see the pain etched on her face and when he'd entered the kitchen a few moments ago, she'd looked as if the whole world were resting on her shoulders.

'You're probably right,' Shay responded, combing her hand through her hair.

'I had hoped to continue our . . . conversation,' Reeve said, but at the grimace of pain that flitted across her face, he knew her headache was worse than she was letting on. 'It's bad, isn't it?' Reeve asked, and almost smiled at the surprised look in her eyes when she met his. 'I'm a doctor, remember?'

Shay managed a weak smile. 'I don't think I'm up to any more conversation, at least not right now.'

'Have you taken something for the pain?' Reeve asked.

'Aspirin. Thanks,' Shay added, touched by his concern.

'Then I suggest you go to bed,' Reeve said. He hesitated before continuing. 'I hope you'll give some thought to what I said. Maybe tomorrow night after the children are in bed, we can pick up where we left off.'

Before Shay could reply, the doorbell rang throughout the house.

'Excuse me,' Shay said. Moving past Reeve, she made her way to the front door. On the doorstep stood a man in his forties, a tired and anxious expression on his face. 'I know it's late, but we were wondering . . . '

'Are you looking for accommodation?' Shay asked, summoning up an encouraging smile.

'Yes,' came the reply.

'Then you've come to the right place,' Shay said. 'I have several rooms available.'

'That's wonderful.' The relief in his tone was almost palpable. 'My wife Helen and I forgot all about the fishing derby this weekend and every motel in town is full,' he explained. 'A lady at the drugstore suggested we try here, but we thought the inn had closed.'

'I only re-opened for business recently,' Shay said. 'It's a little off the beaten track, and not that well known, but I'm hoping to change things,' she added, pleased to learn that someone in town had mentioned the inn. 'There's just the two of you?'

'Yes.' He offered his hand. 'Eric Jefferson.'

'Shay O'Brien. Welcome to O'Brien's Bed and Breakfast Inn.' Shay shook his outstretched hand. 'My rates are reasonable and breakfast is included. I can show you to a room, or perhaps you want to bring your wife in to take a look.'

'I'll get my wife,' he said. 'But I'm sure it will be fine.'

A few minutes later, Shay led the way

up to the second floor, relieved to note that the door to Reeve's room was closed. The Jeffersons appeared pleased with their room, and after giving them a key and telling them the times for breakfast, Shay wished them a pleasant good-night.

The aspirin had taken the edge off the throbbing pain in her head, but the longing to crawl into bed and close her eyes was still tugging at her. Returning to the kitchen, she switched off the lights and finished locking up. She popped in on Mandy and after kissing her sleeping daughter, picked up the kitten and returned her to her bed in the kitchen.

In her room, she undressed and climbed into bed, but sleep evaded her. Lying in the dark, Shay's thoughts returned to Reeve's startling proposal. He'd asked her to think about it, but she already knew what her answer would be.

★ ★ ★

The week that followed proved to be one of the busiest for Shay. The Jeffersons stayed on several days and, to Shay's surprise and pleasure, by late Tuesday afternoon the remainder of the rooms in the inn had occupants.

From a business point of view, Shay was thrilled at the turn of events which helped fill both her days and evenings. Between caring for the girls and looking after her bed-and-breakfast customers, there was little opportunity for a moment alone with Reeve or a chance to continue the conversation he'd started on the evening of the fishing derby.

Although she sensed Reeve's frustration, he hid it well and each evening, as was his habit, he continued his practice of spending time with his daughters, and over the course of the week worked to fulfill the promise he'd made to Mandy to put a roof on the tree house.

With the weekend fast approaching, Shay knew that Reeve would undoubtedly double his efforts to talk to her, and while she wasn't exactly looking forward to the conversation, she also knew she couldn't avoid him forever. Time was running out.

By lunchtime on Saturday, the Dundas family, who'd arrived midweek, were the only patrons still staying at the inn. Shay had promised to take Mandy and Emma to the beach for the afternoon and was packing her beach bag in readiness, when the telephone rang.

'Shay, it's me,' Reeve's deep resonant voice danced across her nerve endings, sending tiny ripples of awareness chasing down her spine.

'Hello, Reeve,' she said on a shaky breath.

'I called to let you know I'll be a bit late getting back this afternoon,' he said.

'No problem. Things have finally quieted down around here,' she told him. 'I promised to take the girls down to the beach for a couple of hours.'

'Good idea. Listen, Shay, I know it's

been a hectic week, but we're running out of time,' Reeve said. 'We need to talk.'

Shay felt her heart leap into her throat at his words. 'Yes,' she agreed after a brief hesitation.

'I don't suppose that's a 'yes' to my solution, but rather a 'yes' we have to talk,' Reeve teased, though there was no mistaking the edge in his voice.

Shay's pulse picked up speed and she tightened her hold on the receiver. 'You're right, we have to talk,' she restated, sounding calm and in control, when, in fact, her heart was racing.

Reeve's sigh down the line told of his frustration. 'That much at least we agree on,' he said. 'It has to be tonight, Shay. We have to settle this before my father and Alice get back tomorrow, before Emma and I leave — '

'I know,' Shay cut in, trying unsuccessfully to ignore the pain suddenly squeezing her heart at the mention of his departure. She was tempted for a moment to tell him her decision over the phone, but she held back, feeling he deserved to hear her answer in person. 'We'll talk tonight,' she said.

'I look forward to it,' Reeve replied.

Shay replaced the receiver and let out a sigh. He wasn't going to like her answer, that much was plain, and she knew he was bound to argue her decision and try to change her mind. She would have to be strong and not let her heart rule her head.

'Can we go now?' Mandy asked a few minutes later when Shay stepped out into the afternoon sunshine, her beach bag and blanket in her hands.

'Yes, we can go now,' Shay said. 'I'm sorry about the wait, but all my chores are done now and I'm taking the rest of the afternoon off.'

'Yeah!' the children chorused.

There were a number of tourists relaxing on the beach enjoying the warm afternoon sunshine, including the Dundas family. Shay waved and smiled at the Dundas children, Natalie who was seven and Peter who was ten.

After spreading out her blanket, Shay removed the pink terry-cloth cover-up she was wearing atop her navy-and-white-striped bathing suit and, kicking off her sandals, challenged the girls to a race to the water.

For the hour that followed, Shay devoted every moment to the girls, trying in some small fashion to make up for the times during the week she'd had to deny them a treat or had pressed them into helping her.

She helped them build a sand castle, played hopscotch on the wet sand, as well as a game of tag running in and out of the water. Mandy invited Peter and Natalie to join them in their game of tag, and as the afternoon drifted by, Shay successfully managed to keep thoughts of Reeve at bay.

Tired and out of breath from the game, the children returned to the sand castle and under Peter's direction began to build a wall around it. Soon, all four children were absorbed in their play, allowing Shay to relax in the sun and watch their progress.

Beginning to feel hot and sticky, she decided to go for a swim, but not before strolling over to ask Peter and Natalie's parents if they'd mind keeping an eye on the girls for her.

On her way to the water, Shay told Mandy and Emma where she was going and the girls nodded and smiled, intent on listening to Peter's plans to dig a moat around their fortress.

The water felt cool and refreshing on her skin and Shay hadn't gone far into the surf before she dived under one of the larger waves, breaking to the surface seconds later, water streaming from her hair and face.

Stroking out farther, she rolled onto her back and began to float, enjoying the silky cool caress of the water as it lapped around her. She closed her eyes, shutting out the bright sun, and as she slowly relaxed, her thoughts turned to Reeve, and ultimately to his offer of marriage.

She had to agree that as a solution it

was a practical one, that the girls would benefit from having both a mother and a father. And watching Reeve with his daughters, seeing the positive way he encouraged and praised them, the warmth and love and respect he showed them, she had to admit that as a father he was first-rate.

But there was something missing from the equation, something she considered vitally important in any relationship and certainly necessary if a marriage was to endure. And that something was love.

Reeve had made no mention of the emotion and while Shay acknowledged that a close family environment was important, the girls deserved more, they deserved two parents who loved each other. And much as she loved Reeve, much as she wanted him, she wasn't the kind of woman to settle for a one-way love affair. She wanted it all.

That's why her answer had to be no. And somehow she had to convince Reeve to leave things status quo. It wasn't something she was looking forward to, and she knew it would be all the more difficult because in a secret corner of her heart she longed to say yes.

Shay opened her eyes and rolling over once more began to tread water. It took her only a second to realize as she gazed at the figures on the beach that in her preoccupation she'd floated out much farther than she'd intended.

Her heart did an unsteady cartwheel in her chest as she tried to gauge the distance back to shore. All at once, a wave crashed over her and for the next few seconds she had to concentrate on keeping afloat as well as try to suppress the panic suddenly clutching at her insides.

The sea was much choppier here and a quick glance over her shoulder told her of another approaching wave. This time she was ready, riding its crest and breathing a sigh of relief as it gently tossed her toward shore.

Her relief was short-lived, however,

when all at once she felt the current pulling her back out again. Her arms were already beginning to ache from the effort and she slowed her actions, trying to conserve her strength.

She could see the children on the beach and wished with a sense of futility that she'd stayed with them instead of going for a swim. When another wave lifted her and tossed her toward the beach, Shay instinctively struck out, taking several strokes that brought her a little closer to shore. Her small victory was soon nullified when she realized that the current was again pulling her back to the point where she'd started.

The water seemed to be toying with her, allowing her to make some progress toward the beach then hauling her back almost to the same spot. She was tiring and she knew it, but resolutely she refused to give up.

Shay gazed longingly at the shore trying to decide whether she could yell for help. Her heart gave a jolt as she watched Mandy stand up and wave at her, and it was all Shay could do to bite back the sob rising in her throat.

Cautioning herself not to waste energy, Shay waved back and, obviously satisfied, Mandy crouched once more to continue what she'd been doing, while Shay fought down the fear and panic threatening to overwhelm her once again.

Suddenly, a larger wave swept over her, pushing her under this time and she held her breath, working with her arms and legs until she finally resurfaced. Her lungs felt as if they were burning and she gulped frantically for air, struggling to regain her composure.

As she fought to steady her breathing, she kept a watchful eye on the approaching waves wanting to prevent a second dunking. Hope surged through her a few minutes later when she noted a large wave heading her way. She gritted her teeth and waited, determined that the wave, coupled with her own efforts, would carry her past the point which so far was proving to be her nemesis.

The moment the wave reached her, Shay began swimming for all she was worth, slicing through the water, silently urging herself on. But minutes later when she stopped to tread water, she felt tears sting her eyes as she discovered that she hadn't achieved her objective, after all, that she was once more being dragged back by the current.

*　*　*

Reeve reached the sand and quickly scanned the beach in search of Shay and the girls. He noticed the blanket spread out nearby and recognized it as the one Shay had used the last time they'd come to the beach.

Closer to the water he saw several children, including Emma, playing in the sand. Dropping his towel and sunglasses onto the blanket, he headed to where his daughter was engrossed in digging a moat around a large sand castle.

'Hi, pumpkin,' Reeve said, dropping to his knees beside her.

'Oh . . . hi, Daddy,' Emma responded, flashing her father a warm smile. 'How do you like the castle we've built?' she asked. 'This is the moat.'

'Wow. It looks pretty impressive,' he responded. 'Hi, Mandy!' Reeve waved to her on the other side of the castle. 'I see you two have found a couple of friends to play with.'

'This is Peter and that's Natalie,' Mandy said, pointing to the other children who smiled shyly at him. 'They're staying at the inn with their mom and dad,' she explained.

'Ah . . . right, I thought I recognized them,' Reeve said. 'Where's your mom, Mandy?'

'Mom went for a swim,' Mandy replied. 'She just waved to me. She's right there, see?' Mandy pointed out into the water.

Shielding his eyes against the sun, Reeve gazed in the direction Mandy was pointing and felt his heart jolt against his ribs in alarm when he saw how far out Shay had swum. Annoyance shimmered through him that she'd ignored his warnings. Surely she hadn't forgotten how dangerous the waters in the cove could be?

Rising to his feet, he continued to watch her and when a wave washed over her and she disappeared from sight for several seconds, he knew she was in trouble. Glad that he'd taken the time to change into his bathing suit on his return to the inn, Reeve shed his shirt and kicked off his sandals.

'I'm going for a swim,' he said, keeping his voice even.

'Okay,' the girls replied in unison, sounding unconcerned.

Reeve strode toward the water. He could see Shay bobbing in the distance. Picking up his pace, he started to run, splashing through the shallow water to dive under a crashing wave. With strong even strokes he began to swim out to her.

With each pull of his arms, Reeve hauled himself nearer to his quarry. Fear and another emotion he couldn't quite define gave added strength to his strokes, but as he cut a path through the waves, he watched in horror as Shay disappeared beneath the surface once more.

Keeping his eyes on the spot he'd last seen her, Reeve swam on, praying for her to resurface. When she reappeared, he could see the look of strain on her face and knew she was close to exhaustion. Intensifying his efforts, he drew closer, fighting down the fear that another wave would reach her before he did.

Shay could see Reeve's figure slicing through the water toward her. Gamely, she kept her arms and legs moving, knowing she couldn't afford to relax her efforts to stay afloat.

An agonizing minute passed, with each second seeming like a lifetime.

Her body ached and every muscle, every nerve, was crying out for her to stop, but she refused to listen.

When she felt Reeve's body skim past hers and his arm close around her chest to pull her against him, she almost sobbed with relief.

'You're all right. I've got you.' Reeve's voice in her ear was like a balm to her soul, but beneath the reassurance she could hear the anger. She managed to nod. Somehow, the fact that Reeve was there with her, holding her, boosted her spirits and gave her strength.

'Let's take the next big wave out of here,' Reeve said. When the next wave hit, they rode it together, and Shay was convinced that only Reeve's strength and grim determination was what brought them past the point of no return.

As the shoreline grew larger and the figures on the beach became clearer, the feeling of relief cascading through Shay was like nothing she'd ever known before. When her feet hit the sand, she tried to stand, but her legs felt like wet paper and she would have fallen if Reeve hadn't scooped her into his arms.

She didn't protest, still shaken by the knowledge of how close she'd come to losing her life. Thanks to Reeve, a tragedy had been averted. What would have happened had he not appeared on the beach when he did? Shay shook her head. It didn't bear thinking about.

The girls came running, anxious expressions on their faces. 'Mom! What happened? Are you all right?' Mandy cast a worried glance at her father as he lowered Shay's legs to the sand.

This time, she managed to stand, but Reeve kept his arm around her waist, holding her steady. Shay was infinitely glad of his support, because she'd started to tremble, both inside and out.

'Your mother's fine,' Reeve answered for her, trying with difficulty to keep a lid on the emotions tearing through him. 'She swallowed some water, that's all,' he explained, his smile reassuring, though it was all he could do not to shout and rage at her.

'Then how come you were carrying her?' Mandy asked, clearly not altogether convinced.

'I felt a little sick and dizzy after I swallowed the water,' Shay said, finding her voice at last although it wavered slightly. She was fighting the urge to weep and the longing to haul Mandy into her arms just to reassure herself.

'Sea water tastes kinda yukky,' Emma commented.

'It sure does,' Shay agreed, holding on to her composure by a slim thread.

'It looks like your new friends are heading back to the inn,' Reeve said, noting that Natalie and Peter's parents had begun to gather up their towels and belongings. 'Emma, why don't you and Mandy go with them? You could show Natalie and Peter the tree house,' he suggested, wanting to engineer a few moments alone with Shay.

Mandy and Emma exchanged quick glances.

'Mom, are you sure you're okay?' Mandy asked.

'I'm fine,' Shay said, summoning up a smile. She wished the children would go, fearful she was going to crumble like a broken doll onto the sand at any minute.

Reeve could feel Shay's body tremble and wondered if she was suffering from shock. Her face was pale but not nearly as white as it had been out in the water before he'd grabbed her. He felt his stomach muscles tense and a pain squeeze his heart as the memory of watching her slip beneath the surface flashed into his mind.

Tightening his hold on her, he gently urged her closer.

'Off you go, you two,' Reeve instructed in a tone that brooked no argument. 'We'll be along in a few minutes,' he added.

Obviously satisfied, the girls nodded and scurried off, calling to Peter and Natalie as they left.

Reeve stood in silence for several

long moments, watching as the children made their way up the beach. From the moment he'd carried Shay from the water, he'd been keeping a tight rein on his anger, but he could feel it gathering force once more.

Grasping her upper arm, he spun her around to face him. 'Now maybe you'd like to tell me just what the hell you thought you were doing swimming out so far?'

Shay could feel the anger coming at her in hot waves and while she understood it and knew she deserved it, she couldn't seem to control the tears suddenly blurring her vision.

'Damn it, Shay! Don't cry!' Reeve said. 'Do you have any idea what it did to me when you disappeared out there?'

Shay heard the pain and anger in Reeve's voice, but the lump of emotion wedged in her throat prevented her from uttering a word.

'You could have drowned!' he continued, exasperation and something more, something she couldn't define, in his voice. 'What were you thinking about? What on earth possessed you to swim out that far? You know how dangerous the water can be in this cove. And what about Mandy? Did you forget you have a daughter? Damn it all, Shay. How could you be so irresponsible? You could have drowned!'

Shay blinked away the tears in her eyes. While she deserved to be raked over the coals for putting her life in jeopardy, she resented Reeve's implication that she'd done it deliberately.

'You're making it sound as if I'd planned to get trapped out there,' Shay countered, anger edging her tone. 'I assure you it wasn't intentional. I was just floating, enjoying the water when all at once I realized I'd gone too far. I made a mistake.'

'You're going to have to do better than that,' Reeve retorted. 'You know this cove like the back of your hand, or at least you did. What the hell were you thinking about?'

'You!' she snapped. 'I was thinking about you,' she said, surprised that he was still angry. She'd never seen him like this before. His eyes were glittering pools of rage, and she couldn't for the life of her understand why he was continuing to make an issue out of the incident, not now the crisis was over.

'Oh, so now it's my fault, is it?' he challenged.

'That's not what I said,' Shay retorted, annoyed and frustrated by his attitude. 'Look, Reeve. I made a mistake. I'm sorry. Can't we just forget it?'

Reeve tensed and she felt a shudder race through him. 'I don't think I'll ever be able to forget it.' Reeve's voice vibrated with an emotion she didn't recognize.

Shay laughed nervously, puzzled by his tone and wishing desperately she could somehow defuse his anger. 'If you keep this up, you'll have me believing you actually care about me,' she said in an attempt to lighten the mood. 'And we both know that's not true,' she hurried on.

The silence that followed her words was electric. Reeve's grip on her upper arms tightened and she watched in fascination as his eyes narrowed and his glittering gaze zoomed in on hers. 'What did you say?' he asked, his voice little more than a whisper.

Shay swallowed, feeling as if she was back out in the water, struggling to stay afloat. 'Ah, that you don't care about me,' she faltered.

'Don't care about you!' Reeve cut in, his voice rising once more. 'Damn it, woman, you're the only woman I've ever cared about.'

Shay stared at him in openmouthed astonishment. Muttering an oath, Reeve hauled her into his arms and brought his mouth down on hers. It's what he'd been aching to do ever since he'd carried her out of the water, because only when he was touching her, tasting her, feeling her respond to him, could he finally begin to push out of his mind the horror of what had almost happened to her.

Never again did he want to relive those terrifying moments in the water, those moments when he'd had to hold back the scream suddenly clawing at his throat, those moments when he'd watched her slip beneath the surface of the water.

It was as Shay disappeared from sight a second time that he'd realized with dazzling clarity that he loved her, had always loved her. And as the truth slammed into him, it had spurred him on to greater effort, and helped propel him closer, ever closer, to where he'd last seen her.

When she'd reappeared, struggling vainly to stay afloat, the relief he'd felt had rocked him. That's when he'd doubled his efforts to reach her and only when he'd had his arms around her, only when he'd felt her body sag against his, had he fully realized how close he'd come to losing her . . . a second time.

Reeve's mouth was hungry on hers demanding a response she was eager and willing to give. But she felt totally and utterly confused. Had Reeve really told her she was the only woman he'd ever cared about?

What did it mean? What did it mean? The question was spinning around inside her head making her dizzy. Or was it Reeve's kisses that were making her dizzy?

She wasn't sure about anything anymore. No, that wasn't true. She was sure of one thing, Reeve was the only man she'd ever loved, and she wanted to stay right here, in his arms, forever.

Reeve broke the kiss and banked the fires raging through him. He held her away from him and looked deep into her eyes. 'Tell me you feel it, too, Shay,' he said huskily. 'I know that after what happened in the past I don't deserve a second chance. I walked away from you once before. But I'll be damned if I'll do it again. But I must know . . . tell me — ' His voice cracked.

'I love you, Reeve,' Shay said softly and sincerely. 'I always have. I always will.'

Reeve closed his eyes and sent up a silent prayer of thanks. Gathering her close, he bent his head and touched his mouth to hers in a kiss that was achingly tender. 'And I love you. I think I've always known it. I knew it ten years ago, but I was just too stubborn, too selfish, too stupid to admit it. Can you ever forgive me?'

'There's nothing to forgive,' Shay said, scarcely able to believe what was happening. 'We both made mistakes. And neither of us was ready for the kind of commitment it would have taken to make things work. We probably would have ended up hating each other. And, besides, if we had gotten together then, you wouldn't have Emma.'

Reeve was silent for a long moment. 'You're right,' he said. 'I can't even begin to imagine what my life would have been like without her. I love my daughter . . . *both* my daughters,' he amended. He kissed her nose. 'Which brings me to the question I asked a week ago. I need your answer, Shay. Will you marry me?'

Shay felt her heart stumble against her breast at the wealth of emotion and the hint of vulnerability she could hear in his voice. She drew a steadying breath. 'If you'd asked me for my answer this morning, I would have said no,' she told him, daring to tease.

'And now?' Reeve asked, his gaze intent, his tone serious.

'Well . . . ' Shay pretended to ponder the question, but her attempt to torment was sabotaged when his mouth claimed hers in a kiss that was powerful, persuasive and much too brief.

'Yes! Yes!' she sighed against his lips and was instantly rewarded for her answer when his lips captured hers once more.

Suddenly, they heard shouting, and Reeve reluctantly broke the kiss, mumbling something about untimely interruptions.

'Mommy!'

'Daddy!'

The voices were closer now. Sliding his arm around Shay to keep her at his side, they turned to greet the girls.

'Daddy, were you kissing Shay?' Emma asked as she came to a halt in front of them.

'Yes, I was,' Reeve confessed.

'I told you they were kissing,' Emma said to Mandy.

'I knew they were kissing,' Mandy replied.

'Do you mind that I was kissing your mother?' Reeve asked Mandy, curious to know the answer.

'If my mom doesn't mind, why should I?' Mandy replied.

Reeve had to bite back the rumble of laughter threatening to escape. He glanced at Shay. 'Shall I tell them?'

'Tell us what?' Emma was quick to ask.

He turned to Mandy. 'Well, your mother and I — ' He stopped and turned to

Emma. 'Shay and I are going to get married.'

'You are?' the girls chorused, grinning at each other.

'Yes, we are,' Reeve confirmed.

'That means you'll be my dad,' Mandy said.

Reeve released Shay and crouched to face Mandy. There would be time enough, he knew, to tell her the truth but right now he simply wanted to try to convey some of the love he felt. 'I hope that's all right with you, Mandy. Because I would be very happy and very proud to be your father,' he said. At his words, tears welled up in Mandy's eyes and his heart ballooned with love.

'I . . . I'd like that a lot,' Mandy said, smiling through the tears. 'As long as it's all right with Emma,' she added, casting a glance in Emma's direction.

'We'll be a family,' Emma announced. 'And we'll be real sisters. Neato!'

'Will we have to move to New York?' Mandy directed the question at Shay, but it was Reeve who answered.

'No, we're going to set up house right here in Stuart's Cove,' he said as he stood up, noting the look of surprise that appeared on Shay's face.

'But . . . I thought . . . What about your new job at Manhattan Metro?' Shay was quick to ask. 'I don't want you to give it up, not for me.'

'I'm not giving it up,' Reeve told her. 'I never accepted it. Having Emma on a full-time basis changed everything for me. My priorities are different now, and I don't need a job that's going to take me away from my wife and family.'

'But you can't start up a medical practice here and compete with your father,' Shay urged.

'I don't intend to compete with him. My father's been thinking of retiring. You heard what Alice said about finding someone who's willing to move to Stuart's Cove,' Reeve said. 'I'd say I'm the perfect candidate, and nothing would make my father happier than if I were the one to take over the clinic.'

'But — '

'Enough!' Reeve said before silencing her once more in the most effective way he knew.

'They'll be doing that a lot, won't they?' Emma said.

'It's what married people like to do, I guess,' Mandy replied.

'Well . . . I don't mind if you don't mind,' Emma said, echoing her sister's comment earlier.

Reeve chuckled softly. 'And I hope you won't mind, either,' he whispered against Shay's mouth, deepening the kiss before she could reply, secure in the knowledge that he would have a lifetime to prove it.

THE END

We do hope that you have enjoyed reading this large print book.

Did you know that all of our titles are available for purchase?

We publish a wide range of high quality large print books including:
Romances, Mysteries, Classics
General Fiction
Non Fiction and Westerns

Special interest titles available in large print are:
The Little Oxford Dictionary
Music Book, Song Book
Hymn Book, Service Book

Also available from us courtesy of Oxford University Press:
Young Readers' Dictionary
(large print edition)
Young Readers' Thesaurus
(large print edition)

For further information or a free brochure, please contact us at:
Ulverscroft Large Print Books Ltd.,
The Green, Bradgate Road, Anstey,
Leicester, LE7 7FU, England.
Tel: (00 44) 0116 236 4325
Fax: (00 44) 0116 234 0205

Other titles in the
Linford Romance Library:

BOHEMIAN RHAPSODY

Serenity Woods

Elfie Summers is an archaeologist with a pet hate of private collectors. Cue Gabriel Carter, a self-made millionaire. He invites Elfie to accompany him to Prague to verify the authenticity of an Anglo-Saxon buckle, said to grant true love to whoever touches it. And whilst Gabriel's sole motive is to settle an old score, Elfie just wants to return to her quiet, scholarly life — but the city and the buckle have other ideas . . .